Hank knew the precise instant Lizzy came back to town.

He could feel her presence. The air seemed to crackle with electricity. And that old familiar ache in the region of his heart started up again.

Still, call it masculine ego or sheer muleheadedness, Hank wanted Lizzy to come to him.

Oh, he knew, sure as shooting, that she'd been avoiding him all these years. He'd seen her blush after she'd kissed him on the eve of her departure. He'd also seen her quick rise of anger and pride when he hadn't tried to stop her from leaving.

Little did she know what letting her go had cost him....

Hank knew—had always known—that he wanted more from Lizzy than a brief, passionate fling. And for that, she had to come to him. In her own time. On her own terms.

Dear Reader,

During this holiday season, don't forget to treat *yourself* special, too. And taking the time to enjoy November's Special Edition lineup is the perfect place to start!

Veteran author Lisa Jackson continues her FOREVER FAMILY miniseries with *A Family Kind of Gal.* All THAT SPECIAL WOMAN! Tiffany Santini wants is a life of harmony away from her domineering in-laws. But there's no avoiding her sinfully sexy brother-in-law when he lavishes her—and her kids—with attention. Look for the third installment of this engaging series in January 1999.

And there's more continuing drama on the way! First, revisit the Adams family with *The Cowgirl & The Unexpected Wedding* when Sherryl Woods delivers book four in the popular AND BABY MAKES THREE: THE NEXT GENERATION series. Next, the PRESCRIPTION: MARRIAGE medical series returns with *Prince Charming, M.D.* by Susan Mallery. Just about every nurse at Honeygrove Memorial Hospital has been swooning over one debonair doc—except the R.N. who recalls her old flame's track record for breaking hearts! Then the MEN OF THE DOUBLE-C RANCH had better look out when a sassy redhead gets under a certain ornery cowboy's skin in *The Rancher and the Redhead* by Allison Leigh.

Rounding off this month, Janis Reams Hudson shares a lighthearted tale about a shy accountant who discovers a sexy stranger sleeping on her sofa in *Until You.* And in *A Mother for Jeffrey* by Trisha Alexander, a heroine realizes her lifelong dream of having a family.

I hope you enjoy all of our books this month. Happy Thanksgiving from all of us at Silhouette Books.

Sincerely,

Karen Taylor Richman
Senior Editor

Please address questions and book requests to:
Silhouette Reader Service
U.S.: 3010 Walden Ave., P.O. Box 1325, Buffalo, NY 14269
Canadian: P.O. Box 609, Fort Erie, Ont. L2A 5X3

SHERRYL WOODS

THE COWGIRL & THE UNEXPECTED WEDDING

Published by Silhouette Books
America's Publisher of Contemporary Romance

SILHOUETTE BOOKS

ISBN 0-373-24208-5

THE COWGIRL & THE UNEXPECTED WEDDING

SHERRYL WOODS

Whether she's living in California, Florida or Virginia, Sherryl Woods always makes her home by the sea. A walk on the beach, the sound of waves, the smell of the salt air all provide inspiration for this writer of more than sixty romance and mystery novels. Sherryl hopes you're enjoying these latest entries in the "And Baby Makes Three" series for Silhouette Special Edition. You can write to Sherryl or—from April through December—stop by and meet her at her bookstore, Potomac Sunrise, 308 Washington Avenue, Colonial Beach, VA 22443.

ADAMS FAMILY TREE

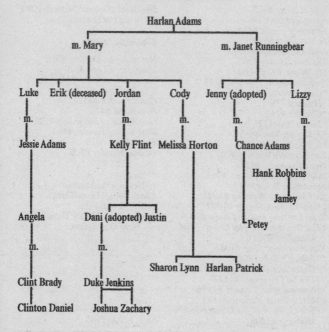

Harlan Adams

m. Mary — m. Janet Runningbear

m. Mary:
Luke — Erik (deceased) — Jordan — Cody

m. Janet Runningbear:
Jenny (adopted) — Lizzy

Luke m. Jessie Adams
Angela
m. Clint Brady
Clinton Daniel

Jordan m. Kelly Flint
Dani (adopted) Justin
Dani m. Duke Jenkins
Joshua Zachary

Cody m. Melissa Horton
Sharon Lynn Harlan Patrick

Jenny m. Chance Adams
Petey

Lizzy m. Hank Robbins
Jamey

Prologue

Lizzy gazed at the grades posted for her anatomy exam and sighed. A lousy *C.* In all of her twenty-four years, she'd never gotten below a B on any test. Studying was second nature to her, cramming for exams as natural as breathing. She'd known the material inside out, but on the day of the test her mind had been somewhere else, not on bones and body parts.

Nothing, *nothing* about the past weeks of her first year in medical school had gone right. The classes had been the most challenging and fascinating she had ever taken, but she'd faltered more than once on exams she should have aced, like this one. It was a lack of concentration, pure and simple, and she knew why.

Her roommate regarded her with a sympathetic expression. "It's only because you've been worried about your dad," Kelsey said. "You'll do better once you've seen for yourself that he's doing okay."

That was part of it, Lizzy agreed. When she should have been memorizing anatomical details, instead her thoughts had been straying to her father.

Harlan Adams had had a mild heart attack the week before, too mild to require her to come back to Texas, too serious to let her concentrate on her studies. All she could think about was the upcoming spring break and her scheduled visit to the family ranch so she could see for herself exactly what shape her father was in. She wouldn't put it past him or her mother to keep the truth from her, if they thought it would worry her when there was nothing she could do to change it.

The huge Adams family revolved around her father. Though he was in his eighties now, none of them could imagine life without him. This heart attack had been a warning that he wasn't invincible. She'd heard the stunned shock in the voices of each of her older brothers when she'd spoken to them. Her older half sister, Jenny, had been even more transparent. Jenny, who wasn't afraid of anything, was clearly terrified at the prospect of losing their father.

In the end, despite his irksome meddling, Harlan Adams was the force that guided all their lives. And even though he'd hated seeing his youngest—the surprise of his life, he liked to say—go off to Miami to medical school, he'd done what needed to be done to pave the way. Lizzy would always be grateful to him for that, for letting her go her own way.

He hadn't been so easy on his sons or even on Jenny, who'd been fourteen and hell-bent on self-destruction when he'd married her mother. He'd forced Luke, Jordan, Cody and Jenny to fight for their chosen careers, putting up roadblocks and hurdles that would have daunted them had they been less determined. Lizzy had been prepared to do the same.

She'd begun by using her wiles as his "baby girl" and then dug in her heels as a typical Adams. Not even the formidable Harlan Adams had had the strength to stand in her way. As much as she loved ranching and despite a whole rebellious year during which she'd experimented on the rodeo circuit, medicine had always held a special place in her heart.

Maybe it had something to do with all those TV shows she'd devoured—reruns of the old *Marcus Welby, M.D.* and *Ben Casey* series, hot new series like *ER* and *Chicago Hope*—shows that had made medicine seem every bit as thrilling as a few seconds on a bucking, bareback horse. She'd thought about medicine all through her undergraduate days at the University of Texas, volunteered at a nearby hospital to soak up the atmosphere, and taken a premed program, just to prove to herself that she'd chosen wisely.

Only one man could have made her change her mind, she thought with a predictable surge of very complicated emotions. Rancher Hank Robbins had

had the power to sway her decision way back when she'd first left for college, but he hadn't. He'd wished her well and waved goodbye as if she'd been no more than a casual acquaintance.

Even now, years later, tears threatened as she thought of how easily that particular man had let her go even after the impulsive, passionate kiss she had initiated had proved just how badly he wanted her to stay. Maybe he'd only meant to do the honorable thing, but rejection was rejection and it had hurt more than she could say.

And yet, if she was to be totally honest, she couldn't help feeling at least a trace of gratitude that he, like her father, hadn't stood between her and her dream. He'd been twenty-four then, the same age she was now, and already he'd been wise enough to see she needed to test her wings.

Still, in all the years since, she'd been careful to avoid Hank. Embarrassment over that kiss was only part of it. Stubborn pride had kicked in, too. But the bottom line was something else entirely. She was afraid, a flat-out coward, in fact. To be honest, though, she wasn't sure what she feared most; that he might not let her go a second time…or that he would.

Yet she couldn't be back home for long without wondering about him. She was pathetically eager for any mention of him, any hint of gossip about his activities. And every time his name came up in conversation, she was terrified that it would be in connection with a wedding announcement. She'd found she could accept with relative calm the news of his being seen with this woman or that. It was only the repeat of the same woman's name that stirred a wellspring of anxiety deep inside her.

It was all ridiculous, of course. In almost five years away, she'd dated dozens of men herself. After the first couple of years when she'd stared at an old snapshot for hours on end, lately she'd gone for entire weeks without once picturing Hank's rugged features or wishing she could hear the low, seductive sound of his voice.

Eventually, she had buried the snapshot in the bottom of a dresser drawer and rarely took it out deliberately. When she stumbled across it, though, her heart always lurched, the pain as fresh as it had been five years ago. Schoolgirl crush or not, she had idolized the cowboy next door.

And all it ever took to resurrect the memories of that long-ago and very much unrequited love was the thought of going home. She'd been thinking about Hank nonstop for the past few days, ever since her mother had called to tell her about her father's heart attack.

The two men were so much alike, despite the decades of difference in their ages. Stubborn, strong men, both of them. Men with staying power. Men capable of powerful emotions and guided by a deep-rooted sense of honor.

So, the truth was, Kelsey was only partially right about Lizzy's thoughts being on her father, instead of concentrating on her exams. In addition, she'd been wrestling with the thorny question of what to do about Hank Robbins, how to—or even if she could—shake the hold he had on her. She'd finally concluded that there was only one way to get Hank permanently out of her thoughts. She had to swallow her pride and see him again. This time she wouldn't avoid him. This time she'd discover if the attraction was still alive.

Maybe then she would be able to put Hank Robbins behind her once and for all, get her medical degree and begin practicing in some big city so far away that she'd never be reminded of him at all. Maybe then she would be able to stop comparing every man she met to the one who'd gotten away.

Or maybe things would get a whole lot more complicated, she conceded candidly. More fascinating, yes. She recalled the way his lips had felt on hers, the way his arms had felt around her. Definitely fascinating. But there was a price for fascination, a whole Pandora's box of complications.

"Lizzy, are you okay?" Kelsey asked, her brow over her thick horn-rimmed glasses knitted with concern. "You're not really worried about this grade, are you? It's a tiny blip on your academic record."

Lizzy forced a smile. "I'm fine," she insisted, setting out for the chemistry lab. "One more exam to go, and then I'm out of here."

Unfortunately, the chemistry exam had nothing to do with the hormonal tug-of-war between a man and a woman. In her current state of mind, she could have written lengthy essays on that particular subject.

On a more optimistic note, it was a written test, rather than a practical exam. The way her mind was wandering, if she'd had to conduct experiments, she very likely would have blown up the whole blasted building.

Chapter One

"Lizzy's coming home," Cody Adams said casually as he and Hank sat on a fence rail between their properties.

Hank had no difficulty at all keeping his expression impassive. He'd had lots of practice over the years at pretending that he had no interest whatsoever in Lizzy's comings and goings. Unfortunately, Lizzy's big brother had his own opinion of Hank's fascination with his baby sister and he used almost any opportunity to taunt Hank about it.

"For how long this time?" Hank inquired, keeping his tone every bit as neutral as Cody's. Most of Lizzy's visits had been whirlwind affairs during which he'd never once caught a glimpse of her. He suspected that was deliberate on her part. He also had no reason to think this time would be any different.

In fact, he'd long since come to terms with the fact that keeping his distance from Mary Elizabeth Adams was the wisest thing he could do. The woman had a way of clouding his thinking, of making him want things he had no business wanting if he expected to turn the run-down ranch he'd bought into a respectable neighbor for the Adamses' White Pines operation. Besides, Lizzy wasn't interested in being a rancher's wife. She had her own dreams.

"A couple of weeks, I suppose. Whatever spring break is these days," Cody said.

"I see. I imagine she's been anxious about Harlan."

"That's part of it, I'm sure." Cody grinned. "Then again, I don't think Daddy's the only reason she's coming."

"I'm sure she misses all of you," Hank said, ignoring the blatant innuendo in Cody's remark.

Cody chuckled. "Give it up, Hank. You're not fooling anyone. Why don't you ask what's really on your mind?"

"Which would be?"

"When she's coming home for good."

"She's not," Hank said flatly. "She made that clear way back. She's going to be a hotshot, big-city doc. From the day I bought this place, all she talked about was her fancy office and her fancy patients."

Cody shook his head. "For a smart man, you are the dumbest son of a gun I've ever met."

Hank refused to take offense. "Thanks," he said dryly. "I've always held you in high regard, too."

"Can't you see that all that talk about setting up practice far away from Los Piños was so much nonsense? All she wanted was for you to ask her to stay. One little sign from you, and she'd be back here in a flash."

Hank wished he could believe his friend, but Cody was every bit as capable as his daddy of wishful thinking. "Did she ever once say that?" he demanded. "Or are you into mind reading now?"

"It's as plain as day," Cody insisted. "Always has been. Don't you think it's time you did something about it?"

"Me? Not a chance. I don't intend to tangle with a woman who's got her mind set on a certain path for her life, especially when that path takes her far away from Los Piños. I chose to be here. She couldn't wait to get away. She'd just end up resenting me, and then where would we be?" He shook his head. "No. This is for the best. Lizzy's smart and ambitious. She'll get the life she wants."

"Paths have a way of coming to a fork," Cody advised him. "Leastways that's what Daddy always says. Maybe when Lizzy hits that crossroads, you could help her decide which way to go. It's always been plain that you have more influence over her than the rest of us. Even Daddy admits that, though it clearly pains him to think that he can't control her."

"I don't think so," Hank said. "That's just Harlan

dreaming up a new way to get what he wants and using me in the process.''

Cody regarded him knowingly. "Are you saying you aren't already half crazy in love with Lizzy?''

"I'm saying that it doesn't matter whether I am or I'm not," Hank said impatiently. "I'm not what she wants.''

"A hundred bucks says otherwise," Cody taunted.

Hank stared at the older man, whose own kids were about the same age as his baby sister. He wasn't sure he'd heard Cody right. It had sounded an awful lot like he was actually daring Hank to make a pass at Lizzy.

"You're betting me to do what?" he asked cautiously.

"See Lizzy, flirt with her, see where it leads. If she blows you off, I'm wrong and you win.''

"And just how far am I supposed to carry things to win this bet?" Hank asked. "I don't want you and Luke and Jordan chasing after me with a shotgun.''

"Not that far," Cody retorted with a hard glint in his eyes and a harder edge to his voice.

"See what I mean. You all would have my hide if I actually pursued your baby sister. You chased off every other man around these parts who was interested in dating her.''

"It wasn't the dating we were concerned about," Cody said, his temper visibly cooling. "Besides, even though you're too stubborn to admit it, I know you care too much to ever hurt her.''

"I'd say your logic is twisted," Hank retorted,

torn between anger and laughter at the pure foolhardiness of Cody's plan. "You want me to put my heart on the line, then be glad of the hundred bucks you'll give me if your sister tells me to take a hike?"

"Then you're admitting your heart would be at stake," Cody said with a hoot of triumph. "I knew it. Daddy said so, too."

"I suppose he put you up to this, too. Well, it's wishful thinking on your part and Harlan's. I'm not admitting a damned thing," Hank corrected. He allowed the weight of his words to linger, before adding impulsively, "But what the heck, you're on."

He wasn't going to admit it to Cody, but he'd been looking for an excuse for a very long time to see Lizzy Adams again. Maybe there'd be fireworks. Maybe there wouldn't. But it sure would break up the monotony of his unceasing thoughts on the subject of the pretty little gal he'd let get away.

"Will you get that danged stethoscope away from me?" Harlan shouted at Lizzy. "You're my daughter, not my doctor."

"I just want to see for myself how you're doing," Lizzy protested.

She'd been home less than a half hour and so far she was no closer to knowing exactly how her father was doing than she had been back in Miami. The only certainty was that he was every bit as cantankerous as ever.

He scowled at her, daring her to put the stethoscope anywhere near his chest again. "You got a degree yet?"

"No."

"Then keep that thing away from me."

Lizzy sighed and put the stethoscope back in her medical bag. "I don't suppose you'll let me take your pulse, either."

"You think I don't know why you've been clutching my wrist every few minutes since you walked in the door?" Harlan grumbled. "If you haven't found the pulse by now, I must be dead."

Lizzy resigned herself to getting a complete picture of her father's medical condition from his doctor and not firsthand. She leaned over his bed and hugged him, relieved by the strength with which he hugged her back.

"What're you checking for now?" he grumbled as he released her.

"That was a daughterly hug, nothing more," she reassured him.

He regarded her warily. "You sure about that?"

"Absolutely."

"Okay, then. Sit down here and tell me what you've been up to. Don't leave out any of the juicy stuff, either. Have you found yourself a man yet?"

She should have known it wouldn't take long to get to the subject nearest and dearest to his heart. "Daddy, not every woman needs a man in her life," she explained for the thousandth time, even though she knew she was wasting her breath.

"Don't give me that feminist hogwash. How're

you going to give me any grandbabies if you don't find a man?''

"Maybe I'll just have them on my own," she taunted because she knew it would irritate him. Clearly, he was well enough to argue. He was probably well enough to be out of bed, too. His wife Janet had hinted that he was playing invalid just to entice his baby to stay around a little longer. If his doctor confirmed that, Lizzy was going to drag him out of bed by force and put him on a regimen of exercise that would have him pleading for mercy.

She shot him a deliberately innocent look and added, "I think I'd make a terrific single mom, don't you?"

"Over my dead body!" he shouted.

"You keep losing your cool like that, and you will be dead," she informed him mildly.

His gaze narrowed. "You said that on purpose, didn't you?"

Lizzy grinned. "Yep."

"Daggone it, girl. You know my heart's weak."

"I don't know that," she reminded him plaintively. "You won't let me check it."

He scowled at her, then said casually, "Cody saw Hank Robbins the other day."

"Really?" Getting that word out without betraying any emotion was harder than tangling with her daddy over the state of his health.

"He said Hank was asking about you."

Lizzy's heart did a little tap dance of its own. "Oh? How is he?"

"Getting along right good," Harlan said. He shot her a sly look. "Cody says he's thinking of getting married and settling down."

This time her heart plummeted straight to her toes. "Married?"

"You sound surprised. Ranch life's a whole lot easier if there's a woman you love by your side. Besides, he's not getting any younger. I'm sure he wants kids."

"I suppose," she said as her heart thudded dully. "Who's he marrying?"

"I didn't say he had anyone special in mind, just that he was thinking of it."

Lizzy stared at her father's innocent expression and chuckled. She should have known he was up to something. "You did that on purpose, didn't you?"

He grinned. "Yep. Worked, too." His expression sobered. "Why don't you just break down and see the man, Lizzy my girl? You know you want to. You were always crazy about him. For a few years there, you were thick as thieves. It made me hope that you'd settle down right next door. I never did figure out what happened between the two of you."

"Nothing happened." Which, of course, was the whole point. She stood up and leaned down to kiss her father's weathered cheek. "Stop manipulating, Daddy. I'd already planned to see Hank while I'm here."

His expression brightened. "Whooee! It's about time you showed some sense."

"Daddy! Don't make too much of this."

"Okay, okay. You going to see him today?"

"I don't know when I'm going to see him."

"Don't waste too much time. Spring break's short." He regarded her wistfully. "Or were you thinking of sticking around?"

"Daddy," she pleaded.

"Okay, okay," he said again. "I'm an old man. I'm allowed to indulge in a little wishful thinking."

"Don't pull that old-man garbage with me. You're going to outlive all of us. You're too ornery not to."

"Sooner or later, age catches up with all of us." He caught her hand in his and clung to it. "Don't let life pass you by, Lizzy. I know you love medicine, but I know something else, too. You've always had a soft spot in your heart for that man up the road. Don't pretend you don't, not with me. I'm just saying whatever you do, don't wake up one day with regrets."

"I told you I was going to see him, didn't I?"

"No need to get defensive, darling girl. I can't help doing a little prodding. It's my nature."

Lizzy sighed. "It surely is." She leaned down and planted a kiss on his forehead. "Now, get some rest and leave Hank Robbins to me."

Harlan Adams grinned, the color in his cheeks getting better every second. "Something tells me the poor man doesn't stand a chance."

"Maybe you're overestimating my charm. Hank didn't have a bit of trouble saying goodbye when I went off to Austin to college or down to Miami for med school."

"Maybe he was just wise enough to let you go after what you wanted. That's not the kind of thing you should blame a man for. In fact, maybe you ought to take a good hard look at what it cost him to let you leave."

Lizzy touched a finger to his lips to silence him. "You're overselling, Daddy. I already know what a paragon of virtue Hank Robbins is. I fell for the man when I was sixteen years old and he bought the old Simmons place. Nothing's changed in the eight years since."

"Then what are you waiting for, girl? Go find him and tell him straight-out what you want."

"I suppose you know what that is, too," she said, wishing she had so few doubts. Loving Hank had been complex enough years ago. Now, with medical school convincing her that she'd chosen exactly the right career for herself, loving him had gotten a whole lot more complicated.

"You want a husband and babies," her father said without hesitation.

"If only it were that simple," Lizzy murmured.

"What was that?"

"You left out medicine, Daddy. I want to be a doctor, too."

"So? You won't be the first doctor to get married and have babies."

"You seem to forget that I have to finish medical school, an internship and my residency. Do you think Hank's going to wait all that time? You've already said he's in a hurry to have a family."

"Darlin' girl, that's what compromise is all about."

Lizzy hooted at that. "What do you know about compromise?"

"Hey, your mama and I don't agree on every little thing. We work things out."

"I'll remind you of that the next time you're trying to bully her into letting you have your way." She squeezed his hand again. "Now get some sleep. I'll be back to see you later."

"After you've seen Hank, right?"

Lizzy rolled her eyes and left the room without answering. She found her mother lurking in the hallway.

"How much did you hear?" Lizzy asked.

"Enough to know that he's trying to marry you off before you go back to school," her mother said with a rueful smile. "Thank you for not arguing with him too ferociously."

"What would be the point? He knows I want to see Hank. He's just trying to make sure I do it on his timetable. There's nothing new about that."

"No, that's your father, all right. When he gets an idea into his head, he can't wait to set it into motion."

"That's how he got you to marry him, isn't it?" Lizzy reminded her. "He wheedled and cajoled and finally wore you down."

Janet Runningbear Adams chuckled. "It wasn't a case of wearing me down," she insisted. "I fell in love with him too quick for that to be necessary. I just held out to keep him on his toes.''

"That's not the way Jenny tells it,'' Lizzy said. "She says the two of them had to conspire to get you to walk down the aisle.''

Janet winked. "And I've always let them think that. It gives me a good bit of leverage around here. Now come on into the living room and tell me all about school and Miami. Did you know I went there a couple of times when I was married the first time and living in New York? Jenny's father liked to go there on vacation, but from all I've read, it's changed a lot over the years. In those days, there were still old people rocking on the porches of those hotels in South Beach. Now, if the pictures I see are to be believed, the place has been overrun with sexy models in bathing suits and in-line skates.''

Lizzy grinned. "That's not so far off, but can we talk about it at supper? I'd like to go for a ride. It's been way too long since I've been on a horse.''

"Of course it can wait. Are you going to see Hank?''

"You, too?''

"Sorry.'' Her mother studied her intently. "Well, are you?''

Lizzy shrugged. "I'm not sure. I suppose I'll make up my mind while I'm riding.''

"Well, in case you decide that the answer's yes, Cody tells me Hank is working in his south pasture today. You know, the one that conveniently butts up against ours. I believe he's replacing a fence that

Cody swears was just fine the last time he checked it.''

''I'll remember that.''

''Be back by suppertime,'' her mother reminded her. ''The whole family's coming for dinner to welcome you home.''

''I'll be back,'' Lizzy promised.

''Bring Hank, if you like.''

''If I see him.''

''Oh, something tells me you'll see him,'' her mother said. ''Can I just add one piece of advice to whatever your daddy's been telling you?''

Lizzy paused in the doorway. ''What?''

''This isn't a game, Mary Elizabeth. While you've been gone, the rest of us have been left to watch Hank. The man's been miserable without you, but he's gotten by. Unless you're really sure about what you want, don't start something up with him.''

Lizzy looked her mother squarely in the eye. ''I was never the one who was unsure, Mom. Hank didn't just let me go. He practically pushed me out the door. You all seem so all-fired sure that he wants me, but he's never once given me any evidence of that. How come nobody seems worried that I'm the one who's going to wind up hurt?''

''Because you've always been able to pick yourself up and dust yourself off, just the way the song says. And maybe because you're the one who's going to walk away in a couple of weeks.'' She gave Lizzy a penetrating look. ''Aren't you?''

''Yes,'' Lizzy said quietly. No matter how things

turned out when she saw Hank Robbins again, she was going to be on that flight back to Miami. She sighed heavily. "Maybe I won't go for that ride this afternoon, after all. I think I'll go on up to my room and unpack. I've got some thinking to do."

"The answers aren't in your room," her mother argued. "Something tells me they're out in Hank's south pasture."

Lizzy grinned at her beautiful mother. Janet Runningbear Adams's Native American ancestry had grown more pronounced as the years lined her face. Her straight black hair was streaked with gray now, but her eyes sparkled with intelligence and wisdom.

"Now who's trying to manipulate me?" Lizzy teased. "You've been with Daddy way too long." Her expression sobered. "He really is going to be all right, isn't he?"

Her mother met her gaze evenly. "If he takes it easy and stops sneaking into the kitchen for ice cream when I'm not looking. I'm thinking of having the refrigerator padlocked."

"It won't do a bit of good. He'll just find somebody in the family who'll sneak things in for him."

"You're probably right. I caught Harlan Patrick taking cigars up to him the other day. He swore he'd just forgotten to take them out of his pocket, but Cody's boy never could lie worth a darn. You should have heard your daddy when he found out I'd confiscated the things."

"When did Daddy start smoking cigars?"

"When he found out he shouldn't. He puffs on

one every now and again just because he knows it makes me furious.''

Lizzy chuckled. "He does know how to rile you, doesn't he?"

"Oh my, yes."

"Mom, I'm sorry I wasn't here when he got sick and that I couldn't get back right away."

"Oh, sweetie, don't feel bad about that. You have a right to live your life. And neither of us wanted you to take time off from your studies when we knew everything was going to turn out fine. Of course, your father and I both wish you were closer to home and that we could see you more often, but we're proud of you. Taking on medical school is a big deal. We know you're going to be a fine doctor."

Lizzy thought of the grades she'd gotten on her last exams. "I wish I had your confidence."

Her mother regarded her with concern. "Troubles with your classes?"

"Nothing to worry about," Lizzy reassured her. "I'll get a grip on things once I get back."

"I'm sure you will. Now, go. If you're not going for a ride, get some rest before supper. You'll need it to fend off all the nosy questions. Your brothers and Jenny may complain about Harlan's meddling ways, but they've inherited the tendency."

Lizzy retreated to her room, which remained exactly as she had left it, with the ruffled curtains and rodeo posters, an admittedly incongruous mix that pretty much summed up her personality.

Instead of unpacking, though, she went straight to

the window seat and settled back against the mound of pillows, staring out across the rugged terrain, imagining Hank out there somewhere, his skin bronzed by the sun and glistening with sweat.

Tomorrow, she thought. Tomorrow she would face him and find out if anything at all had changed between them. With luck she wouldn't be able to stand the sight of him. She sighed at the improbability of that. With better luck, he would sweep her into his arms and tell her he couldn't live without her. Now that, probable or not, was something worth waiting for.

Chapter Two

A man could only mend the same fence so many times without looking like a darned fool, Hank thought as the sun beat down on his bare back. Cody Adams had passed by twice the day before just to get in a few taunts about the obviousness of his activity and to keep him updated on Lizzy's whereabouts.

Even if Cody hadn't told him, though, Hank was pretty sure he would have known the precise instant Lizzy was back at White Pines. He could feel her presence. The air seemed to crackle with the electricity of it. And that old familiar ache in the region of his heart started up again.

"Just come to dinner at White Pines tonight," Cody had suggested. "You know you'd be welcome. The whole family will be there."

"I know that," Hank said.

He liked the whole Adams clan, from Harlan on down. They'd always made him feel like one of them. The littlest rascals in the family were so used to his presence, they had even taken to calling him Uncle Hank. He'd liked the feeling of belonging and he'd enjoyed spending many an evening with them since buying his ranch, but this was different. This time Lizzy would be there, and he didn't know what kind of welcome to predict from her, not when they'd parted on such uneasy terms.

"Another time," he said, covering his regret.

"She won't be here forever," Cody had reminded him. "And we have a bet."

"It's her first day home. There will be time for me to make good on that ridiculous bet."

Call it masculine pride or sheer muleheadedness, but what he didn't say was that he wanted Lizzy to come to him, that he wanted to know that she'd missed him at least enough to finally seek him out.

Oh, he knew as sure as shooting that she'd been avoiding him all these years. He'd seen the flush of embarrassment in her cheeks after she'd kissed him on the eve of her departure for college. He'd also seen the quick rise of anger and pride when he hadn't tried to stop her from leaving. She'd been so sure he would, so confident that that kiss would make a difference. He'd seen that, too.

Little did she know what letting her go had cost him. That unexpected kiss had turned him inside out. No woman had ever made him want so much. And no woman had ever been so far out of reach. The distance was far greater than the miles between Los Piños and Austin or even the miles between home and Miami. They were separated by their dreams.

His were simple. He wanted a wife and children and a small ranching operation that he could take pride in having built from the ground up. The Triple Bar was his. There was no history or conditions tied to it, the way there would have been if he'd stayed at his daddy's place. In that, he was a whole lot like Luke Adams, the oldest of Harlan's sons.

Lizzy's hopes and ambitions were more complex and all-encompassing. Harlan Adams had laid the world at the feet of his baby daughter, and she had embraced it all. Hank wasn't sure she could ever be happy with a life as quiet and self-contained as the one he could offer.

He knew—he had always known—that he wanted more from her than a brief, passionate fling. And for that, she had to come to him in her own time, on her own terms. He'd long ago accepted the fact that she might never come at all.

Knowing that, he'd turned Cody's invitation down, then spent a miserable night back at his own ranch, cursing the day he'd ever met the pretty little sixteen-year-old who'd gone and grown up into a beautiful, willful woman who'd twisted his heart into knots. No man should have to contend with loving a woman like that and watching her walk away.

Today he was back in the same pasture, doing the same work all over again, hoping to catch at least a glimpse of her. What kind of fool did that make him? He'd been asking himself that since sunup and he didn't like the answer any better now than he had hours ago.

Hopefully, Cody wasn't spreading the word about what a pitiful spectacle Hank was making of himself. When he glanced up a few moments later, he thought he was seeing things. There was Lizzy Adams strolling across his pasture looking very much at home and pretty as a picture in her snug jeans and bright red shirt, her black hair streaming down her back under a big black Stetson. Right at this second, with that long, athletic stride of hers, she was a cowgirl through and through. He could almost make himself believe she hadn't changed at all.

Nor, unfortunately, had his reaction to her. His blood heated as if she'd done a whole lot more than offer him a smile and a wave. He was glad then that he'd waited to see her, glad that this first meeting wasn't taking place in front of all those prying, hopeful Adams eyes.

She looked confident and sassy and so damned tempting that Hank clutched the posthole digger a little tighter to keep from dragging her straight into his arms and giving her a proper—well, improper, actually—welcome.

Lizzy didn't seem inclined to show the same restraint. Her pace never even slowed as she sashayed toward him, lifted her hands to his cheeks, gazed straight into his eyes and planted a kiss on him guaranteed to fell a saint. The woman never had hesitated to take what she wanted. Her daddy had always led her to believe that it was her due.

There was hunger and passion and maybe even a little greedy desperation in that kiss on his part and hers. She smelled of sunshine and some kind of exotic flower and she tasted just the way he'd remembered with a hint of mint on her breath. They were both trembling and breathless by the time she pulled away.

"Damn," she murmured, her expression shaken.

Hank grinned. He knew precisely how she felt, as if the ground had shifted under their feet when everyone had declared the earthquake safely past. He dredged up his sense of humor to keep from revealing how shaken he, too, had been, how eager he was for more.

"Was it everything you remembered?" he taunted.

She scowled up at him. "Oh, go to hell."

"Now, that's a fine way to greet an old neighbor."

"The kiss was the greeting. The rest was regrets."

He laughed at that. "I know exactly what you mean."

She regarded him suspiciously. "You do?"

"I was kinda hoping I'd gotten it all wrong, too. Care to try again, just in case the first time was an accident?" The question had nothing to do with his bet with Cody and everything to do with his longing for further experimentation. He'd spent too many restless nights dreaming of having this woman back in his arms. The discovery that she still fit him like the other half of a carved piece of wood was too tempting to resist.

Lizzy shook her head as if to clear it. "No, please. Once was enough to prove the point."

"Coward."

"Me?" she protested. "If you thought the last kiss was all that great, where have you been for the past five years?"

He liked the disgruntled attitude and decided to spur it on. "Comparison shopping," he said.

She frowned at that.

Hank clung to the tiny hint of jealousy. "According to your family, you haven't exactly been living in a cocoon," he accused, immediately proving that he was just as capable of envy. Every mention of a man in Lizzy's life had set acid to churning in his gut, though until now he'd been good at hiding it.

"True."

He studied her speculatively. "So, Miss Lizzy, what do we do now? Wait another five years before we try it again?"

She considered that, her expression thoughtful as her gaze locked with his. Heat sizzled in the air. Finally she shook her head. "Pick me up at six."

Hank's pulse kicked up like an unbroken horse at the touch of a saddle. "For?"

"I wish I knew," she said with a sigh. "Trouble, more than likely."

"Now, Miss Lizzy, I do like the sound of that," he retorted.

"Don't go getting any wild ideas, cowboy," she said, and started to clamber back over the fence.

Hank wasn't ready to see her go. Not yet, not even with the promise of a whole evening ahead of him. "Lizzy?"

"Yes?"

"If you're not busy," he said oh so casually, "why don't you stick around?"

"Why?" she asked bluntly. "You need some help with this fence? Word is it was just fine before you started tampering with it."

He winced at the direct hit, but pressed on. "Actually, I was hoping you'd join me for lunch. I brought a couple of extra sandwiches, just in case you happened by."

Her expression brightened. "Ham and cheese?" she asked, eyeing his saddlebags with a gleam in her eyes.

"On Mrs. Wyndham's home-baked pumpernickel bread," he said, knowing she would find that—if not him—irresistible.

"Did you bring pickles, too?"

"A whole jar."

She was pawing through the saddlebags in an instant. When she'd plucked the thick, foil-wrapped sandwiches from them, her face lit up.

"I've dreamed of Mrs. Wyndham's sandwiches," she admitted as she moved to a spot in the shade of a huge old cottonwood. "I've been in a lot of delis the past few years, but none of them has gotten it quite right. Your housekeeper ought to be declared a national treasure.''

"It's the bread," Hank said, taking a spot beside her and stretching his legs out in front of him. "I don't know what she puts in it, but the taste can't be matched.''

"How'd you remember that I loved these so much?''

If only she knew how many times he'd sifted through the memories of every moment they'd ever shared. After all, she'd trailed after him for years, pestering him with questions and as time passed and she grew into a woman, blistering him with looks hot enough to sizzle steak.

"I remember a lot of things," he said quietly, his hat low so she couldn't read his expression.

"Such as?''

He could pretend, as he had done so many times in the past, treat the question dismissively, or he could tell the truth. Maybe it was time for a little straightforward honesty between them.

"For one thing, the way your eyes light up with golden sparks when you take the first bite," he said, tilting the hat back and keeping his gaze on her steady. "The way your tongue darts out to lick the mustard from your lips. The way you always save one bite as if you can't quite bear to finish.''

She blinked and swallowed hard, but it was Hank who looked away first. If he started cataloging all the rest of the things he remembered about Lizzy, they'd waste the whole afternoon and his blood would be in a heated frenzy.

"How's med school?" he asked, forcing a neutral tone into his voice. This was safer ground, turf that would remind him of all that stood between them still.

"Okay."

"Still getting straight As?"

"Not this quarter," she said.

He heard the rare insecurity in her voice and wondered at it. "How come? Is it tougher than you expected?"

Even as he asked it, he wondered if he wanted the answer to be yes, wanted med school to be so tough that she'd give up on it and come home. But of course, Lizzy was no quitter and coming home a failure wouldn't sit well with her. That was no way to get what he wanted, and he knew it.

"Not so tough. I just haven't been able to keep my mind on my studies the way I should the past few weeks."

"Since Harlan's heart attack?" he guessed, knowing how that would have thrown her. He'd almost called her then to offer support or sympathy or, just as likely, to finally hear the sound of her voice again. That was what had held him back. He hadn't fully understood his own motives, and that was dangerous with a woman like Lizzy.

She nodded, then faced him, her green eyes with those dazzling flecks of gold now clouded with worry. "Do you know how he is?" she asked. "I keep getting the feeling that nobody's telling me the whole truth.''

He wanted to smooth away her frown, but settled for a teasing comment intended to do the same job. ''Hey, you're the budding doctor. Couldn't you tell by looking at him that he's doing okay?''

''He looks good,'' she admitted. ''But he wouldn't let me examine him.''

Hank chuckled at her disgruntled tone. ''I'm surprised you didn't wrestle him down and do it anyway.''

''Believe me, I was tempted.'' She regarded him thoughtfully. ''And you haven't answered my question, either. How is he?''

''What did your mother say?''

''Hank, you're being as evasive as the rest of them,'' she accused.

''I'm just saying if you want answers, the best people to ask are those around him, not me. Your mother doesn't lie to you, does she?''

''No, but—''

''No *but*s. What does she say?''

''That he's recuperating nicely and he'll be fine if he takes it easy.''

''Well, then, that's your answer.''

''No,'' she said, clearly unconvinced. ''He should be up and about by now. You know Daddy. He never was one for sitting still for more than a minute.''

''Maybe he's just hoping to get a little sympathy from his baby girl.''

''Maybe.''

He could tell that she still wasn't reassured. "You're really worried, aren't you?"

"Not worried," she said slowly, lifting her gaze to his. "Scared."

He saw now what he should have seen all along. "You're scared of losing him?"

Tears welled up in her eyes and came close to breaking his heart. She nodded.

"The others have all had him for a long time," she said in a choked voice. "Not me. Twenty-four years isn't nearly long enough."

Hank reached out and brushed away the tear that was tracking down her cheek, barely resisting the temptation to pull her into his embrace and comfort her. "Something tells me Harlan will be around a long time yet."

"Is that guesswork or wishful thinking?"

"Oh, I don't think he's going anywhere until he's had a chance to dance at your wedding. It wouldn't be like him to give up before getting his way."

A smile trembled on her lips. "He does seem to be fixated on getting me married off and pregnant. You'd think all those grandbabies and great-grandbabies already overrunning the place would be enough to suit him."

"But none of them belong to his precious baby girl," Hank countered. "You were the surprise and the blessing of his life. Naturally, he wants to see you settled."

"Whose side are you on?"

"Yours, of course. Always have been."

She regarded him with an unblinking gaze. "You have, haven't you? Even when you thought I'd lost my mind for running off and getting on the rodeo circuit."

"Now, that one did take a few years off my life," he said, recalling the heart-in-his-throat moments she'd put him through every time she'd climbed onto a bucking horse. "But nobody's ever been able to change your mind once you got something into your head. I figured it made more sense to make sure you could stay on a horse than to fight you."

"If it had been up to Cody, Jordan and Luke, they would have locked me in my room until I came to my senses," she recalled, grinning. "You and Daddy were the only ones who didn't try to stop me."

"What would have been the point? You'd have climbed out the window."

She leaned back against the trunk of the tree and gazed around, then sighed. "Do you have any idea how much I've missed all of this?"

"Not enough to come home for more than a minute at a time the last five years," he retorted.

Her gaze locked with his. "You noticed? I'd wondered if you had."

"I noticed," he said.

"You didn't exactly burn up the phone lines between here and Austin or here and Miami."

"Did you want me to? I thought the whole point of going away was so you could try your wings away from all the overprotectiveness around here, mine included."

"Maybe it was, at the beginning," she conceded. "Rebellion seems to be one of those Adams traits." Her lips curved. "But I missed this. I missed—"

Hank held his breath.

"—you," she said softly, as if she were testing it. "I missed you."

Damn, but it was good to finally hear her say the words. But missing wasn't loving. It wasn't saying that this time she'd stay and make a life with him. He couldn't put his heart on the line for that. "I missed you, too, kid."

She glared at him, just as he'd known she would. "Kid?"

Hank winked. "You're still younger than me."

"Oh, yeah. What are you now? Pushing sixty, right?"

"Not even half that, smart aleck."

"Twenty-nine isn't all that old, Hank." She looked him over with a deliberately provocative gleam in her eyes. "Looks as if you have a few good years left in you, if you'd work a little to get yourself in shape."

"What's wrong with the shape I'm in?" he demanded. "It can't be all that bad. You've been ogling me since you came out here."

"Have not."

"Have, too."

She chuckled. "Listen to us. We're back to bickering the way we used to."

"Some things never change."

"I wish nothing had to change," she said with a sigh.

He sensed the shift in mood went beyond the bickering of two old friends. "You're thinking of your father again, aren't you?"

She nodded, then forced a smile. "But all the worrying and wishing in the world won't change things."

"Have you talked to his doctor?"

"Not yet."

"Then go. Do that this afternoon. Maybe it'll put your mind at ease." He touched a finger to her cheek, watched the color bloom at the light caress. For an instant, her gaze clashed with his and he thought for sure she was going to turn her face ever so slightly and press a kiss to his palm.

But she drew in a deep breath and shot to her feet instead. "I think I will go see the doctor."

"Still want me to pick you up at six?"

She gave him a sassy grin. "Unless you're having second thoughts."

"Oh, no, darlin'. Where you're concerned, I've always had a one-track mind."

Hank's words lingered in Lizzy's head for the rest of the afternoon. There'd been a challenge there, no doubt about it. The man had actually been flirting with her, which had to be a first. She couldn't help wondering whether that was because he'd finally seen that she was all grown up or whether something else was going on. Living with a houseful of manipulators had made her wary of sudden shifts in attitude.

Of course, wariness wasn't enough to keep her home. She was curious to see just where this brand-new attitude would lead them. In fact, now that she'd been reassured by her father's doctor that his heart had suffered no permanent damage, she could devote all of her attention to Hank and figuring out just how much he really mattered to her.

Cody wandered in as she was pacing in the living room, awaiting Hank's arrival.

"Going someplace?" he asked, looking her over, then scowling at the short skirt she'd chosen.

"I have a date."

"With?"

"Hank."

His gaze narrowed. "Is that right?"

"Do you disapprove?"

"Of Hank? Of course not. But you might want to consider adding a couple of more inches to that skirt before you walk out the door."

Lizzy glanced down. "Why? Don't you think he'll like it?"

"Oh, he'll like it. A little too much would be my guess."

She grinned. "Then I got it just right, I think."

Her brother studied her worriedly. "Lizzy, what are you up to?"

"Up to?" she repeated innocently. "I have no idea what you mean."

"Oh, yes, you do. You've got that sneaky-female look in your eyes."

Lizzy laughed. "And what would you know about sneaky-female looks?"

"I'm married, aren't I? Melissa always gets a look just like that in her eyes right before she pulls the rug out from under me. I've watched my own daughter use it on every man she's ever dated, too. Now that Sharon Lynn's engaged, poor old Kyle Mason spends most of his life looking thoroughly bewildered by her. I actually feel sorry for him."

Lizzy gave a little nod of satisfaction. "Then I suppose I've finally got that right, too."

Something that might have been panic flared in her brother's eyes. "Lizzy, I will not have you going out with Hank and doing something you're going to regret."

"Regrets are for people who never took any risks," she retorted.

"Risks?" Cody demanded, his voice escalating. "Just what risks are you intending to take?"

Lizzy heard Hank's car outside and decided Cody had had about all he could take of her teasing. She reached up and patted his cheek. "Don't worry about a thing, big brother. I've got everything under control."

Cody moaned.

Lizzy walked out on him before he could get it into his head to try to run Hank off the property. That was not the sort of trouble she'd intended when she'd made this date. No, if there was going to be trouble tonight, it was going to be between her and Hank Robbins.

She could hardly wait.

Chapter Three

When Lizzy got outside, Hank was exiting his pickup. He almost stumbled at his first glimpse of her. His stunned expression was everything she'd hoped for when she'd chosen the skirt of which Cody so vehemently disapproved.

"Too anxious to wait for me to come in and get you?" Hank inquired, giving her a lazy, purely masculine once-over that raised goose bumps.

"Protecting your sorry hide," she declared, refusing to rise to the taunt. "Cody's into his big-brother mode. If he'd seen you looking me over like that, there's no telling what he'd do."

His gaze strayed to the midthigh hem of her skirt. "I can imagine. That skirt ought to be banned in most parts of the world."

"You don't like it?"

"Oh, I like it," he conceded. "It just changes my plans for the evening."

"In what way?"

"I don't think we'll be dining out in town, after all."

Lizzy chuckled. "Suddenly can't wait to get me alone, huh?" she taunted. She had deliberately—and successfully—provoked one reaction out of him. Now she was working on one far more dangerous.

"Not exactly," he retorted. "I'm just afraid I'd have to strangle half the men in town for salivating over you. Fortunately, Mrs. Wyndham hasn't left yet. I'll call her from the truck and tell her to fix something."

"Sounds good to me," Lizzy said, thinking the evening couldn't have looked more promising.

"You haven't gone and turned into a vegetarian, have you?"

"And have Daddy disown me? I don't think so."

"Then I'll tell Mrs. Wyndham to leave a chicken roasting or defrost a steak or something," he said, still sounding as if he'd been poleaxed.

Lizzy gave him a knowing look, then turned toward the truck and hesitated as she contemplated the long step up to get inside. It was the one thing she hadn't considered when she'd chosen her outfit for the evening. Obviously, she'd been living in the city too long, where flashy cars, not practical trucks, were the norm among the men she'd dated.

"An interesting quandary, isn't it?" Hank inquired, laughter threading through his voice. "Either you ask for help or you scramble up on your own and expose yourself—" he chuckled "—to humiliation."

"A gentleman wouldn't need to be asked," Lizzy declared.

Before the words were out of her mouth, he slipped up behind her. She felt his hands circle her waist and the next thing she knew she had been lifted off her feet and settled snugly into the passenger seat of the 4×4. But Hank wasn't half as quick to release her as he had been to lift her up. His work-roughened hands slid from her waist to settle briefly on her thighs. Her suddenly all too bare thighs.

Lizzy's breath caught in her throat, and heat climbed into her cheeks. Her pulse ricocheted wildly as Hank leaned closer and closer still until his lips were almost on hers. She waited impatiently for him to close the distance between them.

The man had impeccable timing. She'd give him that. Just when she thought her heart was going to burst with longing, his mouth settled over hers, soft and gentle and coaxing. It was nothing like their greedy, frantic kiss that morning. This one was all about subtle nuances and pure temptation.

The kiss lasted an eternity, or maybe it only seemed that way because it stole her breath and left her reeling. If she was over the man, his kisses shouldn't have any potency at all. One should have been pretty much like another.

Instead, they seemed to get more and more devastating. That morning, Lizzy had been thoroughly shaken by the discovery that time hadn't dimmed the power of Hank's kiss to rattle her completely. She was even more shaken by this one, in part at least because he had initiated it. It only confirmed the risk she was taking in seeing him tonight. Somewhere along the way, he'd gone and changed the rules on her.

First he'd openly flirted with her, and now this kiss. Whatever restraints he'd placed on his actions years ago seemed to be a thing of the past. The turnaround was unexpected and dangerous, but it played nicely into her own plans. For once she wasn't going to worry about risks or consequences. She was dedicated only to discovering whether old dreams could be turned into reality.

She suspected they both knew where this date was going to end up. Heck, she'd wanted to throw him down on the ground out in that pasture and make love to him right there. Discovering after all this time that he was not nearly as indifferent to her as he'd always pretended had only heightened her desire. At this rate, they'd be lucky if they made it to the end of the very long White Pines driveway before they started ripping each other's clothes off.

"Hank?"

"Hmm?" he murmured, clearly reluctant to release her.

"Cody's inside. He's probably been watching every move we've made. My hunch is he's halfway between the living room and the gun cabinet."

Hank pulled away and sighed. "I suppose you have a point."

"Believe me, no one wishes it were otherwise more than I do."

"Then I suppose I'll have to be satisfied with the fact that we're only twenty minutes down the road from my ranch."

"We could make it in five, if we took the horses, instead of driving the long way around," Lizzy argued.

He studied her intently. "Surely you can hold the thought a few extra minutes."

Lizzy refused to admit that she'd been clinging to the same thought for years. "I'm not sure. You might have to remind me."

"Not a problem," he said, regarding her with a look every bit as hot as a branding iron. "Not a problem at all."

Hank was pretty sure he was in way over his head. One look into Lizzy's sparkling, expectant eyes, and rational thought fled. He'd always known she wanted him, always forced himself to ignore the blatant desire in her eyes.

Tonight, though, there would be no ignoring the obvious. He had the distinct impression if he tried to exercise a little restraint, Lizzy would take matters into her own hands. Clearly, the woman was out of patience, and he was darned sure out of willpower.

Hank doubted Cody had intended him to seduce Lizzy the first chance he got. He also figured it was none of her big brother's damned business what they did. Lizzy was twenty-four now and certainly knew her own mind, and this had been a long time coming. Not that Lizzy's desires would enter into it for Cody—or any other Adams. If their protectiveness kicked in, Hank was done for.

For once, though, Hank was only going to worry about one Adams, the woman seated beside him with her eyes on the road and her hand resting less than subtly at the top of his thigh.

Lizzy's touch was so intimate, so disturbing that he forgot completely about the call he'd intended to make to his housekeeper. He had to concentrate very hard to keep his eyes on the road or they'd end up in a ditch.

Because of that, they walked into the ranch to find the lights on, but the oven cold and not so much as a whiff of Lizzy's favorite bread in the air, much less the scent of dinner.

"Damn," Hank muttered, gazing around in dismay at the tidied room and bare table. "Mrs. Wyndham's gone."

"Were you feeling the need for a chaperone?" Lizzy inquired.

"Actually, I was more concerned about the dinner I promised you."

She stepped up close and slid her hands up his chest. "Oh, I think we can improvise. I'll bet you know your way around a kitchen."

She might have been talking about cooking, but

Hank got the distinct impression that dinner was the last thing on Lizzy's mind.

Still, he made a valiant attempt to get her to focus. He extricated himself from her clever, wandering hands and aimed for the refrigerator. Maybe a quick blast of chilly air would cool him off sufficiently to keep his wits about him. After all these years of waiting, he didn't want to hurry things along too much. There was something to be said for anticipation, though he'd thought until now that he'd had his fill of it.

"Hank?"

"Yes?"

"Am I making you nervous?"

"Sweetheart, a tornado makes me nervous. You scare the daylights out of me."

She seemed surprised and just a little fascinated by that. "I do? Why?"

Hank grinned at her. "Oh, no. I'm not giving you any ammunition to use against me. You're way too sure of yourself as it is." He deliberately turned back to study the contents of the refrigerator. "How about baked ham?"

Instead of a response, he felt the glide of a hand up his back. His body jolted at the touch.

"Lizzy." It came out in a choked voice, part plea, part protest.

"Yes, Hank."

She sounded amused. Obviously, Lizzy had learned a lot about seduction since she'd been away. Hank wanted to murder the man who'd taught her.

He swallowed hard and forced a nice, neutral tone into his voice.

"I asked if you wanted baked ham."

"I want you."

Well, hell. The game was pretty much up now, Hank thought desperately. He slowly closed the refrigerator door and turned to face her. "Lizzy..." he began, intending to be rational and very, very careful in what he said next.

She cut him off by slanting her mouth over his and snuggling up so tight that his entire body went on red alert. He locked his fingers around her elbows, intending to push her away, but a moan of pure pleasure escaped instead.

She tasted like mint and felt like satin and fire. Hank's ability to fight the potent combination pretty much wilted on the spot. Years of pent-up hunger rampaged through him. There was a brief moment— no more than an instant—when he could have backed away, but as if she sensed it intuitively, Lizzy chose that precise second to slide her tongue into his mouth, to rock her hips against his already throbbing arousal.

Hank was lost. He'd wanted her for so long, dreamed of having her in his arms, in his bed, hot and willing and filled with just this kind of urgency. He broke off the kiss and scooped her into his arms, then headed for the master suite. At the door, he locked gazes with her.

"Are you sure?" he asked, because it was the right and honorable thing to do. Even so, he prayed he already knew her answer, because if she said no now, he was pretty sure his body would shatter into a thousand pieces.

She touched a finger to his lips and smiled. "Stop fretting, cowboy. I've been sure forever."

Hank believed her because he was desperate to. He carried her into the suite and kicked the door closed behind him. Slowly, he lowered her to the king-size bed, then went to pull the drapes across the wall-to-wall glass with its view of the wildflower-bright fields at sunset.

"No," Lizzy protested. "It's beautiful. It will be like making love outdoors." She grinned at him impishly. "Just the way I wanted to earlier today."

"Making love was on your mind this afternoon?"

"Yep," she said without the slightest trace of embarrassment. "How about you? Did it cross your mind when you saw me?"

All this straight-out talk about making love was making Hank nervous, but he couldn't deny the truth. "Oh, yeah, darlin'. It crossed my mind."

She gave a very feminine nod of satisfaction. "Good."

Hank sank down beside her. She had always had a tart tongue and willful nature, but he got the distinct impression that the past few years had given her a new level of confidence to go along with that. Add in the discovery of her own sexuality, and she might very well be more than any sane man ought to tangle with.

"Lizzy—" he began, only to be interrupted before he could get the thought out.

"Hank, surely we did not come into your bedroom to chat," she said, reaching over to fiddle with the buttons on his shirt.

Hank brushed her hands away and tried one more time to focus on having a sensible discussion. "Lizzy, just how experienced are you?"

Her hands, already back at work on his buttons, stilled. She met his gaze evenly. "You want to talk about my track record with men?"

Hank detected a dangerous note in her voice, but he plunged on. "I think we should. Not how many or anything like that. That's none of my business, actually."

"I'm glad you can see that much at least."

He swallowed hard. "I was just wondering…have there been any?"

"I'm twenty-four, Hank. What do you think?"

He thought if she'd run across a man she wanted since leaving Los Piños, she wouldn't have hesitated to sleep with him. The gleam in her eye suggested it would be wise not to suggest that.

"I think," he said softly, "that a straight answer is called for. Your experience or lack of it makes a difference in where we go from here."

"Is this one of those technical discussions, then?" she inquired ever so politely. "To determine if delicate, virgin-appropriate behavior is warranted?"

Heat flooded into Hank's cheeks. "Something like that."

To his astonishment, a smile suddenly broke across her face and she flung herself into his lap.

"If that isn't the sweetest, most caring thing anyone has ever done," she said, peppering kisses across his face. "Next you're going to want to talk about birth control, aren't you?"

Hank sighed. "Yes."

She knelt and straddled his thighs, framing his face with her hands. "Okay, here it is. I have never, ever slept with a man. I am taking birth-control pills. It seemed like the sensible, responsible thing to do. Does that cover everything?"

"Sensible?" He seized on her choice of words. It wasn't a word he would have associated with the impetuous Lizzy. "Were you anticipating—" he hesitated and chose his words carefully "—something like this?"

"I'm twenty-four," she reminded him again. "You never know when the right man might come along."

"I see."

"Hank?"

"Yes?"

"How much longer is this conversation going to last?"

He heard the thread of impatience in her voice, recognized the flare of fire in her eyes. "Oh, I'd say we're pretty much at the end of it."

"And you're not backing out or anything?"

He pulled her to him. "No, darlin'. Not if my life depended on it."

He covered her mouth with his and wondered at the way the taste and feel of her made his pulse jump and his blood heat. Surely other women had had the same effect, but at the moment he couldn't think of a single one who had. Maybe that's what truly scared the daylights out of him. He knew—had always known—that once a woman like Lizzy got into a man's blood, she'd be there forever.

Yet there was no way at all, no way in hell, he could walk away from her now without ever knowing the way her body would come alive at his touch, without tasting for the first time the pebble-hard nipple of her breast, without feeling the slick, moist heat of her surrounding him.

One by one, he stripped away her clothes, allowing himself to feast on the sight of her. He'd seen her in the skimpiest of bikinis, but it wasn't the same as watching her blouse slowly slither away to reveal a lacy, sexy bra in purest virginal white. It wasn't at all like watching her shimmy out of that scrap of a skirt to reveal lacy bikini panties in startling, come-hither red.

Sweet heaven, she was perfect, with her full breasts and narrow waist and hips that flared just enough to entice a man to bury himself inside her. Her skin, when he reached for her, was burning hot to his touch, a wonderfully alluring mix of silk and dangerous fire.

But it was the look in her eyes that captivated him. Part saucy wanton, part innocent, it was the look of a woman with no second thoughts and anticipation very much on her mind. She was his for tonight at least, and he would never forget the precious gift she was bestowing on him.

"You are so beautiful," he said, his voice low and husky. "So very beautiful."

"Am I?" she asked, sounding surprised.

"As if you didn't know."

"Okay, you're not the first person to say it," she admitted. "Just the first one who mattered."

Hank was awed by the implication of that and by the trust she was placing in him. "I've always thought you were beautiful," he told her. "I just wouldn't allow myself to think about it."

"I was so afraid you would never look at me as a woman, that I'd always be the pesky kid next door."

Hank chuckled. "Lizzy, I think you were born grown-up. I never thought of you as a kid—that was the scary part. I used to be terrified someone would take advantage of that."

"But never you," she said softly.

"No," he agreed. "Never me."

"Hank?"

"Mm-hmm."

"I think we've waited long enough."

"Yes, darlin', I think we most assuredly have," he agreed as he removed the last of her clothes and set out to teach her everything he knew about making love.

He was slow and patient and dedicated with his caresses, until the fire burning inside her had her writhing beneath him, her body coated with a sheen of perspiration and jolting with his every touch as she strained toward a first-ever climax.

"Not just yet," he whispered as he knelt above her. "We're going on this ride together."

He entered her then, taking care to be sure that the pain was quick and over almost before she knew it.

"Oh!" she protested, then "Oh, my" as he eased deep inside.

Hank couldn't seem to tear his gaze away from her face as emotions raced across it, from anxiousness to anticipation to pure, ecstatic delight. Then when he was sure that her pleasure was at its peak, he allowed his own to build until they both shattered with soul-rocking climaxes, first hers, then his.

Slowly, slowly, their breathing returned to normal. Hank's heart began to pump at a steadier beat. But, he realized, his desire hadn't waned at all. He knew in that instant that he would never get enough of Lizzy Adams, that the attraction would never wane, only deepen.

Maybe if this night had never happened, eventually he would have found another woman to love, another woman to share his life. Now, though, he knew for fact what he'd always suspected: his life would never be complete without Lizzy in it. Just how in hell they were going to accomplish that was something to contemplate another time, without the distraction of having her curled up next to him, her sweet breath feathering across his chest.

"Lizzy?"

"Hmm?" she murmured.

"Are you okay?"

"Oh my, yes."

He smiled at the disingenuous reply. "Hungry?"

"You mean for food?"

"Yes, for food. It's getting late, and we missed dinner completely."

She sat up and stretched, the unselfconscious movement stirring him all over again. He couldn't seem to drag his gaze away from her body. She looked over at him, noticed his state of arousal and grinned.

"Are you absolutely certain dinner is what you're hungry for?" she inquired.

"I suppose I could wait a little longer," he conceded, reaching for her again.

It was an hour later before they finally left his bed and traipsed into the kitchen. He'd insisted Lizzy wear one of his shirts. "Otherwise we never will get dinner."

"No willpower, huh?" she inquired lightly.

"I think I've displayed amazing willpower over the years. Today's lapse is hardly inexcusable."

Her expression sobered. "Hank?"

He stilled and gazed into her upturned face. "What, darlin'?"

"What happens now?"

The topic was way too heavy and way too complicated for a midnight discussion. Hank sidestepped it.

"Now we get out eggs and scramble them, add a

little ham and cheese and have ourselves a midnight snack.''

"That's not what I meant and you know it."

He sighed. "I know it. I think maybe that's a question we both need to sleep on before we get into it."

"Which raises another subject," she said. "Am I sleeping here tonight or are you taking me home?"

Hank had given the matter some thought already. "Much as I would like to have you stay right here with me all night long, I think the smart thing to do is get you back to White Pines."

"Why?"

"The obvious answer is to keep your brothers from hunting me down with a shotgun, but it's more than that."

"Such as…?"

"I'm not sure we want to stir up a lot of questions before you and I are ready with the answers. Beyond that, I respect your father and mother too much to want to flaunt this in front of them."

She nodded slowly. "I suppose you're right." She regarded him with a hint of uncertainty. "You're not regretting this, are you?"

He cupped her head in his hand and planted a lingering kiss on her lips. "There is no way I could ever regret this. You and I have had this date with destiny a long time now." He studied her closely. "What about you, though? Any second thoughts?"

"Not a one."

"Well, then, let's get out a bottle of champagne and have a toast with our meal."

"Champagne?"

He grinned. "Would you prefer hot chocolate?"

"As a matter of fact, yes," she said, eyeing him with a touch of defiance. "So I'm not a world-class sophisticate. Sue me."

"Hey, there's nothing I like better than a little hot chocolate with marshmallows on top."

"You manage to make that sound incredibly sexy."

"It is. When all that gooey marshmallow winds up on your lips, I get to lick it off."

Lizzy's eyes brightened. "Now, there's an idea. Where are the marshmallows?"

"Over the stove."

He couldn't help noticing that when she reached for them, his shirt rose to an indecent level that distracted him from the eggs he was supposed to be fixing.

"Hank, is that the scrambled eggs I smell burning?"

He glanced down and yanked the frying pan off the burner. "Damn."

Lizzy peered into the ruined mess.

"Maybe you'd better let me fix them this time. You don't seem to be able to stay focused."

"If you had on a few more clothes, it wouldn't be a problem."

She spun around in an exaggerated pirouette. "I don't know. I'm growing rather fond of this look. It makes a definite fashion statement."

"Exactly. It says 'I've just been in bed with a man and I'm going back there at the first opportunity.'"

She chuckled. "Can you think of a better marketing slogan than that?"

"I don't think they need to market sex. It does just fine on its own."

"I was talking about shirts."

"Sure, you were."

"Not everything is about sex."

"It is in this room," he observed. "Now sit down over there and behave. The eggs will be ready in a minute."

She sat, but she bounced right back up. "How about toast? Want me to make toast?"

He scowled with mock ferocity. "Sit."

She grinned knowingly, but she sat once more, only to pop right back up. "Juice. I'd love some orange juice. How about you? Aren't the glasses up on the top shelf? I'll just stretch a little and—"

Hank gave up on the eggs, the meal, everything except Lizzy. He turned off the stove, then scooped her up.

"Whoops," she exclaimed when he swept her off her feet and headed back to the bedroom.

It was 3:00 a.m. when he finally dropped her off at White Pines. Neither one of them seemed to give a darn that they never had had dinner.

Chapter Four

Lizzy would have slept until noon, but the pounding on her bedroom door had her jolting awake at barely seven. The incessant noise pretty much destroyed the good mood she'd been in when she'd crawled under the covers after coming home from Hank's.

"Who the devil is it?" she shouted.

"Justin."

"And Harlan Patrick."

Her nephews, who were virtually the same age she was, had better have a very good reason for hauling her out of bed at this ungodly hour or she was going to scalp the pair of them.

"What do you want?" she demanded, hauling the covers up to her neck and considering whether to bury her head under a pillow to drown out the noise.

"We thought you might want to go for a ride," Justin said, sounding innocent as a lamb. "Unless you've turned into too much of a city girl and forgotten how."

"It's a beautiful morning," Harlan Patrick added.

Neither of the two young men had ever been particularly inspired by the weather before. Lizzy's suspicions were promptly aroused. They had been sent, no doubt by their respective fathers—her big brothers—to pump her for information about her date with Hank.

"Go away."

"You sound sleepy," Justin noted. "Must have been a late date."

"She got home after three this morning," her father chimed in from his suite of rooms across the hall.

Oh, sweet heaven, Lizzy thought, moaning. The whole blasted family was in on the act. Thank goodness she *had* come home, instead of staying at Hank's as she'd desperately wanted to do. He'd been very wise to insist on it.

Obviously, going back to sleep was out of the question. She climbed out of bed and yanked on a robe. Without bothering to wash her face or run a brush through her hair, she yanked open her bedroom door and padded out to join the fray.

"Are you two happy now?" she inquired testily. "Now the whole household's wide-awake and knows the details of my date."

Justin grinned. "Sounds to me like Grandpa Harlan already knows more than we do."

She poked her head in her father's room to find him out of his bed and reading the morning paper in a chair by the window in the sitting room next door. He wasn't even trying to look innocent. She aimed a suspicious look in his direction.

"Which brings up an interesting point," she said. "What were you doing up at 3:00 a.m.? You're supposed to be a sick man."

He winked at his grandsons, then turned to Lizzy. "I'm a light sleeper. You ought to remember that next time you come in humming some cheerful little ditty. Of course, your mama and I certainly did enjoy the entertainment."

"I'll bet it was a love song," Harlan Patrick, Cody's son, taunted with a wicked gleam in his eyes.

"And I'll bet you never inspire a woman to hum a love song, you sorry excuse for a male," Lizzy retorted.

"Children, children," her father chided.

Justin's expression sobered at once. "How're you feeling, Grandpa Harlan?"

"Better now that I've got a doctor in the house."

"That's nonsense," Lizzy countered. "You don't even trust me enough to let me take your pulse."

Harlan Patrick winked at her. "Is that what you were doing till three in the morning? Playing doctor with Hank?"

A fiery blush bloomed on her cheeks. "You are such a pain. You know that, don't you?"

"But I'm handsome and sexy and lovable."

"I can't imagine who ever told you that," she said.

"Laurie Jensen, that's who," Justin retorted, giving his cousin a wink. "Laurie thinks Harlan Patrick hung the moon. And for your information, she has been writing songs about him. She claims one day she's going to make him famous with a Grammy-winning country-music song."

"She'll do it, too," Harlan Patrick said with obvious pride. "The woman does have a way with words."

"She ain't half-bad-looking, either," Justin noted appreciatively. "Wait till you meet her, Lizzy. You won't be able to imagine what she sees in a poor old cowboy like this one."

"Hey, watch it," Harlan Patrick warned. "Just because you don't have a woman in your life doesn't mean you get to pay close attention to mine."

"Would *you all* stop your fussing?" Harlan grumbled. "A man can't get any peace in his own house anymore."

Lizzy dropped a kiss on her father's cheek. "I thought you were sick of peace and quiet."

"I'm just beginning to recognize its advantages," he retorted. "Now, get along with you, all of you. Breakfast's getting cold downstairs." He shot a look at his namesake. "I don't suppose you could slip one of those blueberry muffins up to me."

"No, he could not," Lizzy declared, even as Harlan Patrick gave his granddaddy a conspiratorial wink. She whirled on her nephew. "You will not bring a muffin up here."

"Oh, don't go getting your drawers in a knot, Doc," Harlan Patrick responded. "They're fat free. Everything around here these days is fat free and cholesterol free—"

"And downright boring," her father concluded.

"You mean healthy," Lizzy corrected.

"No, I mean boring. If you knew what I'd pay for some eggs and bacon and home fries, you'd haul it up here yourself."

"Not if I was destitute," she countered. "Now read your paper and rest. It's good to see you out of bed."

"Then you'll be downright thrilled when you find me downstairs at lunchtime," he retorted. "It's about time I had me a face-to-face talk with that housekeeper of mine. Janet won't let Maritza near me because she's afraid I'll pull rank and make the old woman fix me something edible."

That said, he turned his attention back to the paper, dismissing the lot of them.

With her father's bedroom door closed again, Lizzy turned to her nephews. "I'll see the two of you downstairs."

"Don't take too long primping," Justin warned. "Hank's probably getting restless."

"Besides, something tells me the man's so smitten already, he won't care if you're all dolled up or not," Harlan Patrick chimed in.

''What does Hank have to do with this ride we're taking?'' she inquired warily.

Both men grinned.

''What would be the fun of going if it didn't give us a chance to see the fireworks going off the minute the two of you get into close proximity?'' Harlan Patrick said.

Justin added, ''And something tells me the show's going to be better than ever this morning.''

''Daddy told me Hank planned to work up by the creek today,'' Harlan Patrick added. ''Funny how that immediately brought to mind what a lovely spot that would be for a romantic little picnic should anyone special happen to come along.''

''Hasn't anyone ever taught you guys the old expression that two's company and three's a crowd?'' Lizzy muttered, slamming her bedroom door in their faces.

Despite their admonition to hurry, she took her time and primped. She told herself it was just to spite Harlan Patrick and Justin, but the truth was she wanted Hank to take one look at her and remember every steamy, sexy minute they had spent together the night before. She didn't want that famous noble streak of his to go kicking in and call a halt to this relationship before it got off the ground. He'd already been worrying something fierce by the time he brought her home. She'd felt it in the distracted, half-hearted way he'd kissed her good-night.

Thinking about that, she concluded she didn't especially want an audience when she saw Hank this morning. She wanted to be able to indulge in all of her powers of persuasion, which she certainly didn't want reported back to the rest of the family as the kind of gleeful gossip Justin and Harlan Patrick were prone to. The pair of them had spent their teenage years tormenting her about her crush on Hank and about every other date she had. They considered it their duty to be their grandfather's eyes and ears on his baby girl's love life.

She slipped down the back stairs, intending to sneak out through the kitchen, only to find Harlan Patrick and Justin sitting at the kitchen table talking to the housekeeper as they drank their coffee.

"Took you long enough," Justin grumbled.

"Typical woman," Harlan Patrick said.

"Actually, I was hoping you two would be long gone by now."

"And miss out on watching you and Hank dance around each other in some sort of bizarre mating ritual?" Harlan Patrick said. "Not a chance. I can't recall ever seeing two people spend so much time pretending not to be crazy about each other, when it was plain to everyone else how they really felt."

"Boys, stop teasing your aunt," Maritza chided. "In matters of the heart, only the people involved can decide what's for the best."

"But some of them are pitifully slow about figuring it out," Justin commented.

"I wasn't aware there was a timetable," Lizzy retorted. "Maritza, is there any coffee left or have these two finished the entire pot?"

"I have coffee in a thermos for you and saddle-bags packed with warm coffee cake. Enough for two."

Lizzy grinned. "Not four?" She looked at the two men as she took the thermos and headed for the door. "Sorry, guys."

"They have had their share," the housekeeper said. "Along with eggs and toast and home fries and ham."

She paused with the screen door half-open. "Neither of them slipped away during breakfast and carried that same menu upstairs, did they?"

"Never," Maritza insisted. "That is why I made them eat in here, where I could keep a close eye on the two of them. I know they are the ones responsible for sneaking things to your father."

"Uh-oh," Justin said. "We've been busted."

"Hope word doesn't get around when you go off to the police academy," Harlan Patrick said. "You'll never get an undercover assignment."

Stunned by the taunt, Lizzy stared at the older of the two. "Justin?"

He shot her a defiant look. "What?"

"Since when are you not going into the oil business with your father?"

"I decided a while ago," he admitted.

"But he just got around to telling Jordan last week," Harlan Patrick said. "Be glad you weren't around for that explosion."

"I can imagine," Lizzy said. "He always dreamed of turning the business over to you."

"So, he'll turn it over to Dani's husband instead," Justin said, referring to his older half sister. "Duke loves the oil business. He's good at it. Let him sit around and push papers for the rest of his life. I want to be a cop."

Lizzy wasn't sure which startled her more, Justin's choice of a career or his daring to defy his father.

"Even when we were kids, you always wanted to play the good guy," she recalled thoughtfully. "I suppose it makes sense. If Jordan calms down long enough to think about it, maybe he'll see that you came by the notion naturally. He was always a real straight arrow, too."

"Maybe you could mention that to him next time you see him," Justin said. "Not that I need his approval, but it sure would be nice not to walk into an armed camp every time I go through the front door. Poor Mom's caught in the middle."

"How does she feel about you becoming a cop?"

"She's pretty much okay with it, as long as I come back here to work, instead of going to some big city like Dallas or Houston. That scares her to death."

"Will you do that?" Lizzy asked. "Will you come back to Los Piños?"

Justin nodded. "That's the plan."

"He seems to think he knows all the laws around here real well," Harlan Patrick teased, "especially since he broke so many of them."

Ignoring the taunt, Lizzy came back into the room and hugged Justin. "I'm glad for you. Fighting the plans this family makes for us isn't the easiest thing in the world to do.'' She turned to Harlan Patrick. ''You're lucky. You've always wanted to follow in your daddy's footsteps and run White Pines someday. Ranching is in your blood.''

''That and Laurie Jensen,'' Justin taunted.

''Okay, enough,'' Harlan Patrick said, heading for the door. ''Are you two coming or not? I don't have all day to waste sitting around here gossiping like an old woman.''

''Oh?'' Lizzy retorted. ''But you have enough time to come along and spy on Hank and me?''

He grinned. ''Yep. I always make time for the important things. Besides, I promised Grandpa Harlan I'd come back with a full report.''

With that, he took off running, Lizzy right on his heels. ''You'd better be darned glad your legs are longer than mine,'' she shouted after him. ''Because if I catch up with you, Harlan Patrick Adams, you are a dead man.''

''Big talk for a city girl,'' he shouted right back as he mounted his horse.

The two men had saddled Lizzy's horse before she came downstairs so she was able to mount the pretty little mare and take off after Harlan Patrick at a full gallop. Justin muttered a curse, then raced after them.

After the first ten minutes of the high-spirited chase, Harlan Patrick slowed his horse and allowed Lizzy and Justin to catch up. He winked at her.

''Truce?''

She debated making it so easy on him, then nodded. ''Truce.''

"Thank goodness," Justin muttered. "I really wasn't ready for my first homicide investigation."

"But just think what a reputation you would have gotten if your first arrest had been Lizzy," Harlan Patrick noted. "Ordinary folks would have trembled in fear at the sight of you in uniform."

"Okay, okay, fellows, let's not get carried away," Lizzy said. "Nobody's going to die." She gave him a pointed look and added, "Leastways not this morning. And nobody's going to jail. Now fill me in on the rest of the news around here."

"You heard it all at supper your first night back," Justin declared. He shot a sly look over her head at Harlan Patrick. "Of course, there was that one rumor about Hank that nobody mentioned."

Lizzy's gaze narrowed. "What rumor about Hank?"

"That he's got a woman over in Garden City, one he's been seeing real regular."

"Yeah, I hear she's hot, too," Harlan Patrick said.

Lizzy's temper began to heat. "Is that so?" she said softly.

"Now, I ain't saying it's fact," Justin said. "Just that it's a rumor. Of course, you know how talk can get started around here. All it takes is somebody blabbing about something totally innocent, and the next thing you know, trouble's brewing."

"Oh, trouble's brewing, all right," Lizzy said just as Hank came into sight. He was taking a break from whatever work he'd been doing. He'd stripped off his shirt in the morning heat and was leaning back against a tree, his Stetson tilted low over his face.

Lizzy dismounted, stalked straight over to the creek and filled her own hat with icy water, then took it and dumped it squarely over the two-timing sneak. Drenched, he jolted upright to the sound of masculine laughter and hoofbeats. Lizzy whirled and saw that her nephews had taken off, kicking up a storm of dust in their wake.

When she turned slowly back, Hank was regarding her warily. "Mind telling me what that was all about?"

She winced as she watched the water tracking down all that bare flesh.

"If I had to guess, I'd say it was a little practical joke courtesy of Harlan Patrick and Justin."

"Where's the guesswork? You're the one who soaked me. Don't you know why the hell you did it?"

"I did it because of something they told me," she confessed, watching him uneasily. "But judging from the way they took off, I'd have to say now that they probably made the whole wild tale up."

"And what wild tale would that be?"

She would have preferred to avoid getting into that, but Hank's expression warned her not to try dancing around the subject. "Something about you and a woman in Garden City," she admitted reluctantly. "A very hot woman."

Hank nodded soberly. "I see. And you were what? Jealous, maybe?"

"Never," she denied instinctively.

"Oh, really? Then why am I soaking wet?"

"Because…" Her voice trailed off for lack of a plausible explanation.

"Because you were mad as hell that I might be seeing another woman," he teased. "Well, hallelujah!"

"I'm glad you're enjoying yourself so much."

"It's just that I have waited for a very long time for some sign that you gave two figs about what I did with my time. Do you know how many rumors I planted at White Pines every time you were due home?"

She stared at him incredulously. "You planted rumors," she repeated slowly. "To make me jealous?"

He nodded, grinning. "If you counted up, I have supposedly dated at least a dozen women since you left town. I came darned close to playing the wedding march as background music every time I casually dropped a hint about one of them. You have no idea what it did to my ego to have you ignore every single rumor."

Lizzy walked up and jabbed a finger in his chest. "Why you, low-down, sneaky, lying devil," she said as she began backing him up. She came up with a satisfyingly long list of comparisons to reptiles and other forms of lowlife. With each step, an unsuspecting, defensive Hank came closer and closer to the bank of the creek. In the end, all it took was a gentle nudge to topple him straight into the icy water.

The shocked expression on his face was priceless,

but she didn't have much time to enjoy it. The glint in his eyes suggested she just might have overplayed her hand.

"Gotta go," she announced, and raced for her horse.

Just as she loosened the reins she'd looped around a low-hanging branch, Hank gave a sharp whistle and the mare bolted.

"Uh-oh," Lizzy murmured as a dripping Hank strode toward her.

"Uh-oh is right," he said in a silky voice that was more dangerous than a shout.

"Now, Hank," she soothed.

"Don't worry, darlin'. This will be painless," he replied as he reached for her.

"You're all wet," she protested.

"Now, whose fault is that?" He dragged her close, then slanted his mouth over hers, swallowing her screech of dismay.

Then she concluded that it didn't matter that Hank was soaking wet or that the creek had been like ice. Between them, there was enough heat to warm an entire cabin in a blizzard. She was pretty sure there had to be a fog of steam around them.

"Now, then," Hank murmured slowly when he pulled away. "You won't ever, ever try anything like that again, will you?"

Lizzy grinned. "If it's going to turn out like this, I might."

He chuckled. "Obviously, the punishment did not suit the crime. My mistake."

With that, he scooped her up and headed straight into the creek, not slowing until he was waist high and Lizzy was every bit as soaked as he was.

She was sputtering by the time he carried her back to shore. "That was…"

"Yes?"

She heard the dare in his voice. "Memorable," she said finally. "Definitely memorable."

"Good."

"Just one thing."

"What's that?"

"Is there a woman in Garden City?"

Hank hooted. "If there were, do you think I'd tell you?"

Lizzy regarded him suspiciously. "Whose hide would you be protecting? Hers or yours?"

"Doesn't matter. When you get riled, you are a force to be reckoned with."

She gave a little nod of satisfaction. "You'd do well to remember that."

"Duly warned," he agreed, then gave her a once-over that raised goose bumps. "Now, then, why don't we get out of these wet clothes and lay them in the sun to dry?"

"That could take a long time," she noted, her pulse already pounding.

"Indeed, it could."

"What will we do to make the time pass?"

"Oh, I have a few ideas."

She grinned at his expression. "Oh, I'll just bet

you do. I have some nice hot coffee. We could drink that. And have some of Maritza's coffee cake.''

"That wasn't by any chance in your saddlebags, was it?''

She glanced over to where she'd had her horse tethered and remembered the beast's defection. "Never mind.''

"Don't look so sad, darlin'. I think I can make you forget all about that coffee cake.''

"You'll have to work very hard at it.''

"Oh, I intend to,'' he said, beginning to undo the buttons on her blouse. "In a couple of minutes, you won't even remember how we got into this fix.''

His knuckles skimmed across her nipple as he removed her soggy bra. Desire shimmered through her. By the time her clothes were spread out in the sun and his were scattered beside them, there was absolutely nothing on Lizzy's mind but the way Hank's body fit so perfectly with her own.

Chapter Five

For Hank and Lizzy, the pattern established itself quickly and continued for the next several days—a few hours apart, then long, leisurely evenings indulging in the passion they had denied themselves for far too long.

They discovered a lot about each other during those nights. She realized that his feelings for her weren't new at all. Years ago they had been powerful enough for him to understand her dream and to let her go. He recognized that she had grown into a woman capable of giving every bit as much as she took. She was dedicated to the profession she'd chosen, but she was capable of being just as committed to a man.

None of that changed the fact that she was going

to leave, that in a few days she would go back to Miami and back to medical school.

And he would stay behind.

It made their time together bittersweet, but this time Hank clung to the possibilities instead of the doubts. He set out to court her, to show her all of the thousand and one ways he needed her.

He was selfish about it, too. He didn't want to share her for a minute. Their trips into town for dinner were always cut short by the quick flaring of passion, the hunger to be alone and in each other's arms.

Even though he understood the necessity for her going back to White Pines each night, even if it was barely before the crack of dawn, he hated losing even those few sweet hours when they might have been together. To his gratification, she hated it more.

But no matter what arguments she tried, he was adamant. Part of it was respect for her parents. Some of it was a way of clinging to a shred of distance, a way of pretending to himself and to her that their relationship wasn't as all-consuming as they both knew it was.

And some of it, he conceded ruefully, was a way of staving off exhaustion. In bed together, there wasn't a chance in hell either of them would get a wink of sleep.

"Will you be having dinner in tonight?" Mrs. Wyndham asked as Lizzy drove up outside as she had been doing every afternoon by three, the time when Hank cut short whatever work he'd been doing and came inside to shower and change for their time together.

Hank watched Lizzy emerge from the car and managed to draw his attention away from the sight of that slim, lithe body long enough to murmur assent.

"Anything in particular you'd like me to fix?"

"Whatever you think."

"I doubt either one of you will notice," the housekeeper muttered, but there was a smile on her face when Hank jerked around to look at her.

"You're probably right, Mrs. Wyndham," he admitted sheepishly. "But just in case, fix something decadent for dessert. Lizzy has a sweet tooth."

He'd discovered that about her, that and her ready laughter, her razor-sharp wit and the surprising grasp she had of ranching. Why hadn't he realized that being Harlan Adams's daughter meant ranching was in her blood? It allowed him to believe that she would be suited to life here with him, even if it meant foregoing her medical career. He prayed he wasn't deluding himself about that.

She'd certainly seemed contented enough the past few days. The subject of school hadn't cropped up once. He sighed and wondered if maybe it should. A big part of her life had been declared off limits by silent, mutual consent.

Yet when she came rushing through the front door, a smile on her face, Hank didn't have the stomach for hard truths.

"Hey, darlin'," he said, opening his arms to welcome her.

Lizzy fit against him snugly, generating enough heat that only Mrs. Wyndham's presence nearby kept him from making love to her smack-dab in the middle of the foyer. Eyes shining, she met his gaze.

"So, cowboy, what are we going to do tonight?"

"I thought we'd stay in. Do you mind?"

"Are you kidding? There's no place I'd rather be, nothing I'd rather do."

He searched her face intently. "You sure about that?"

"Absolutely."

"There must be friends you've been wanting to catch up with," he suggested. "And your family must be wondering where you've disappeared to."

"I've caught up with all my friends in the mornings, when you've been busy. As for my family, they have a pretty good idea where I've been spending my time."

"And they don't object?"

"Not when you're making me so incredibly happy."

He grinned at that. "I'm sure if it were otherwise, I'd have heard from those overprotective big brothers of yours."

"Exactly right," she said, then gave him a wide-eyed look. "What are you planning to do to keep me happy?"

"I think I'll start with this," he said, lowering his head to steal a kiss.

He meant it to be no more than a teasing brush of his lips, but kissing Lizzy never quite turned out the way he expected. She had a sneaky way of luring him into doing things he'd never intended. He was hot and hard and breathless by the time they broke apart. Not that it took a lot of doing, but she could make him want her with a fierce desperation just by skimming her mouth over his.

Wanting that badly should have terrified him, but he ignored all the warning signs. All he felt was gratitude that she wanted him back. Today, this minute were the only things that mattered. Tomorrow would just have to take care of itself.

"If we don't slow down, we're going to shock Mrs. Wyndham," he said.

"Give her the rest of the day off," Lizzy suggested.

"She's fixing our dinner."

"We can finish," Lizzy said as she unbuttoned a few more buttons on his shirt. "Later."

Hank groaned as her lips touched bare skin. "Much later."

She had worked most of his shirt free when he struggled to regain his composure. "Wait," he murmured with regret.

"Wait? Why?"

"Because I still haven't made it to the kitchen to tell Mrs. Wyndham she can leave."

"Oh. Right." Her gaze locked with his. "Maybe I'll just wait for you in your room."

Hank swallowed hard. "That would be good."

He watched her sashay off down the hall, then shook himself. What was he supposed to be doing? Oh, yeah, giving his housekeeper the night off.

At the doorway to the kitchen, he checked to make sure all his clothes were back in place, then opened the door. Suddenly, he felt like a schoolboy again, trying to put something over on a teacher.

"Mrs. Wyndham."

She glanced up from the pie crust she was rolling out. "Yes, sir."

Hank searched for an explanation that sounded innocent, but not one single word came to mind. "Um, how's dinner coming?"

"It'll be a while yet. It's not even four. I was figuring on getting it on the table at six, like always. Is that okay? Are the two of your hungry now? I could fix a snack."

The kind of hunger troubling them could not be sated with cheese and crackers, Hank thought. Still, he nodded. "Sure, a snack would be great." He glanced around for something that didn't require preparation. "Maybe some fruit," he said, seizing on the sight of a huge pottery bowl of apples, oranges and bananas. "I'll just take this."

He grabbed the bowl and headed for the door. Only when he was on the other side did he realize that the woman was chuckling. So much for discretion. Obviously, he was totally, disgustingly transparent.

When he walked into the bedroom with the fruit, he found Lizzy in the middle of his bed without a stitch of clothes on. The bowl slipped from his grasp, and fruit tumbled every which way. He barely noticed. Thankfully, the pottery was cushioned by the carpet or he'd have been walking over shards of it to get to the woman before him. He quickly shut the door behind him and turned the lock.

"Got a little ahead of me, didn't you?" he asked, his gaze fastened on her bare breasts.

"You looked as if you could use a surprise."

"Honey, a birthday cake is a surprise. This is a shock."

"A shock?" she repeated, sounding suddenly uncertain.

"Not a bad shock," he said hurriedly. "It's just that Mrs. Wyndham is still here."

"You didn't tell her to go home?"

He shook his head. "Afraid not."

"How come?"

"Because it would have been like telling my mother to go away so I could have sex." He shuddered at the thought. His mother was a lovely woman, but she did have her rules about propriety. This situation definitely did not fall within the guidelines. He figured his housekeeper would agree.

Lizzy chuckled. "Hank Robbins, you are shy."

"Not shy, just discreet."

"Which explains all those apples and oranges. Somehow your housekeeper got the idea that we were hungry."

"Starving, in fact."

"Then I suppose you'd better gather them up and

bring 'em over here. You can peel the oranges and feed them to me.'' She winked. ''With any luck, the juice will trickle into all sorts of interesting places.''

''Right,'' Hank said, though he was having difficulty tearing his gaze away from the sight before him on the bed. ''Just one thing.''

''What's that?''

''Do you suppose you could put your clothes back on? I'm having a really hard time concentrating.'' He forced himself to begin the search for apples and oranges. When he had most of the elusive fruit back in the bowl, he backed toward the door. ''I'll just be in my office when you're dressed.''

''I could just slide under the covers and wait until Mrs. Wyndham leaves.''

''Bad idea,'' Hank said.

''You afraid she'll check the room before she goes?''

''No, I'm very much afraid I'll throw caution to the wind and join you. The whole orange-juice image you stirred up was damned inviting.''

''I could live with that.''

He grinned at the declaration. ''Sure. You're leaving town. I'm the one who'd have to live down sending my housekeeper into cardiac arrest when she found the two of us.''

She studied him thoughtfully. ''Maybe it wouldn't be such a bad idea. At least the gossip would warn all the predatory females in town that you're mine.''

''Darlin', there are no females in town you need to worry about,'' he assured her.

"What about Garden City?"

Amused by her continued fascination with the mysterious woman in the next town, he shrugged. "I doubt the gossip would spread that far."

Her gaze narrowed. "Then you're admitting there is a woman there?"

"I'm not admitting to a thing."

"Why won't you tell me?"

"Because not knowing for sure will give you a reason to hurry home."

"Oh, I'll be back in June, all right. And I'd better not hear that you've been roaming over to the next county."

"Or what?"

"Or I'll just have to go over there myself and tear her hair out."

Lizzy sounded so fierce that Hank was very relieved that no such woman existed. He also couldn't help feeling just a bit of smug satisfaction that Lizzy Adams was finally, at long last, pea green with jealousy.

Except for her morning visits with her father over his much-hated bran cereal, Lizzy was beginning to resent every second she had to spend away from Hank. These first days of loving him openly were so precious, she didn't want to waste a minute of them.

Still, there were those times when Hank had to work, anyway. She used those hours to visit with her sister, Jenny, and her nieces, Dani and Sharon Lynn, both of whom were a few years older than she was.

Sharon Lynn was happily planning an oft-delayed, midsummer wedding to longtime fiancé Kyle Mason. This time the two of them were determined to pull off the event. Every previous attempt had been postponed due to one crisis or another. Lizzy had her own opinion about the real reason for the delays, but she would never in a million years have shared them with Sharon Lynn. As long as her cousin was determined to go through with this wedding, come what may, then Lizzy was behind her a hundred percent.

Now, with the absolutely, positively, last-chance, final date practically upon her, Sharon Lynn was so distracted that most of the customers at Dolan's Drugstore were at high risk when they ordered lunch at the counter Sharon Lynn had been running for the past few years. Lizzy walked in just as her niece was about to serve a raw hamburger to the local sheriff.

"I'll take that," she said, swooping in and grabbing the plate before her niece could put it down.

Sharon Lynn gazed at the plate blankly. "Was something wrong?"

Lizzy winked at Tate Owens. "Even old Tate here likes his meat cooked before he eats it," she said as she slapped the burger on the grill. "Why don't you have a seat at the counter, sweetie? I'll rustle up a sandwich for you, too."

"But it's my job," Sharon Lynn protested.

"Which won't last much longer if you keep running off the customers with your offbeat recipes."

Sharon Lynn looked puzzled. "Offbeat recipes? I don't understand."

"You gave Millicent ketchup with her pancakes yesterday and tried to pour soda over Mr. Lincoln's cornflakes," Lizzy said, mentioning only the latest two episodes of forgetfulness that had been described by her father that morning. He was taking great delight in the tales Harlan Patrick was spreading about his sister.

"Then there was the notorious tuna-salad incident," the sheriff chimed in cheerfully. "Jake Conroy's still trying to figure out the sweet taste of that sandwich you served up on a sliced doughnut. Fortunately for you, Jake's eyesight ain't what it used to be."

Sharon Lynn sank down on a stool. "Good heavens. It's gotten that bad?"

"Worse, actually, but nobody's blaming you yet," Lizzy said. "Everybody knows your mind's on your wedding."

"Do you suppose that's why Kyle thought the last milk shake I fixed him tasted like grapefruit juice?"

Lizzy exchanged an amused glance with Tate as she gave him his medium-rare burger. "Could be," she agreed. "I'm surprised he noticed. Word is that he's every bit as muddleheaded these days as you are."

"And I suppose you've never done anything absentminded," Sharon Lynn grumbled. "Just wait. The way things are going with you and Hank, one of these days you're going to walk out of the house without your shoes or with your hair in curlers and wonder why everybody's staring."

"Lordy, I hope not. If I get that distracted, I'll be downright dangerous with a flu shot."

Tate studied her intently. "So, it's true, then? You're going to be a doctor?"

Lizzy nodded. "That's the plan. Of course, I have a long way to go yet. I have to finish med school, an internship and a residency."

"Old Hank must be a patient man," the sheriff noted. He winked at her. "But a darned lucky one. Hope you'll be coming back here and hanging out your shingle one of these days."

His words sent a chill through her. That wasn't the plan at all. And yet, what had she thought was going to happen? Did she expect Hank to abandon his ranch and move to some city with her? Of course not. Which meant either she had to come back to Los Piños eventually or she had to give up the man she loved.

"Well, damn," she murmured, sinking down onto the stool next to Sharon Lynn.

"What is it?" her niece demanded. "Lizzy, what on earth is wrong? Are you sick?"

"Not sick, just stunned."

"Am I supposed to understand what you're talking about?"

"No, of course not." She forced a smile. "I guess I just butted headlong into some hard truths."

"Such as?"

"The fact that Daddy's been fibbing to me all these years."

Sharon Lynn looked shocked. Like the rest of the

family, she was convinced her granddaddy Harlan hung the moon. "How so?" she asked in a voice barely above a whisper.

"He's always told me I could have it all. Now I'm not so sure."

"Why on earth would you say that?"

"Because in order to have Hank, I'd have to give up medicine."

"Don't be ridiculous. You heard Tate. You could practice right here in Los Piños."

"There's not a trauma center anywhere near here."

"Trauma center? Since when did you decide you wanted to do emergency medicine?" She regarded Lizzy intently. "Is it because of that cute actor on *ER?*"

"Don't be absurd," Lizzy said, though her words were belied by the defensive note in her voice.

Sharon Lynn began to laugh. "It is, isn't it? You wouldn't sound so irritated if that weren't it."

"It's because of the volunteering I did in the emergency room when I was in college," Lizzy retorted.

"If you say so."

"I do."

Just then Hank walked up behind her. "Now, there's a phrase I've been longing to hear."

Lizzy whirled around so fast she almost spun herself right off the stool. "What phrase?"

"I do."

She studied his face, searching for a trace of humor, some sign that he was only teasing. His expression was sober as could be. "Careful what you wish for, cowboy."

"Do you want to put my sincerity to the test?"

Lizzy thought about the terrible quandary she'd been pondering just before his arrival and shook her head. "No," she said ruefully.

There was the slightest flaring of disappointment in Hank's eyes, but it vanished almost before she could be sure it was there. He slid onto the stool next to her, then glanced around.

"Who's working around here? Or have you turned this place into a self-service restaurant, Sharon Lynn?"

"It might be better if I had," Sharon Lynn replied as she moved behind the counter. "Apparently, I'm getting to be downright dangerous back here. I'd suggest you stick to something simple, like a soda."

"How about a grilled cheese and fries with it?"

"Don't say you weren't warned," she retorted, and went to work fixing his order.

Hank swiveled to study Lizzy. She winced under the intense scrutiny.

"What's up with you, darlin'?"

"Nothing," she denied.

"You're going to have to do better than that."

She forced an indifferent shrug. "Oh, just thinking about this and that."

"Which one am I, this or that?"

"What makes you think you've been on my mind at all?" She paused. "Wait a second. What are you doing here in the first place? Shouldn't you be working?''

"I'm the boss. I left Pete in charge and gave myself the day off. Then I came looking for you. Your father said you'd come into town. Your mother reported you were over here pestering Sharon Lynn."

"With those tracking skills, you could become a private eye."

"I don't think so. You're the only person I'm the least bit interested in finding."

She regarded him with fascination. "Is that so?"

"That's the honest-to-God truth."

"Interesting. You do realize, of course, that you've just given me an amazing amount of power over you?"

"No, darlin'. The power's always been there." He winked. "You're just now figuring out how to exercise it."

Chapter Six

Hank was pretty sure life didn't get any better than this. His ranch was thriving, but more importantly, the woman he'd been crazy about as far back as he could remember almost seemed to be within reach.

Lizzy was amazing, every bit as surprising and delightful in bed as she was in the other parts of her life. The way she'd taken him on at the creek, when she'd thought he had a lover in another town, brought a smile to his lips every time he recalled it. Okay, it had been fair warning never to cross her, but more importantly, it had also been proof positive that she cared.

That didn't mean he wasn't going to have a thing or two to say to Justin and Harlan Patrick next time he saw them. They'd been careful to steer clear of him ever since their practical joke.

Those two were entirely too full of themselves. They'd always been capable of getting into mischief, but now these were grown-up games they were playing. Once he'd had his say, they wouldn't be pulling any pranks on him again anytime soon.

Then there'd been the eager way Lizzy had fallen in with his afternoon of playing hooky from the ranch. After leaving the drugstore and Sharon Lynn the day before, they'd gone riding, taking along the picnic dinner his housekeeper had prepared for them. They'd eaten on a ridge overlooking his land and hers and watched the sunset splash a golden glow over everything.

Then they'd made love, out there in the open with the sky turning dark and filling up with stars. Just the memory of it was enough to stir his blood.

He was sitting in his office taking care of the monthly bills, when he heard a car skidding to a halt outside, followed by the slamming of a door. His body promptly concluded it had to be Lizzy, even though she wasn't due for a half hour yet. His hormones reacted with predictable anticipation. Just to prove to himself he still had a little self-control, he left it to Mrs. Wyndham to answer the door.

To his deep regret, it was a man's voice he heard talking with his housekeeper.

"Hank, it's Pete," she said, even though his foreman was by then standing right beside her.

"Hey, Pete. I thought you were going to move the cattle today."

"I was, but we've got a problem."

Looking at the older man's face, Hank could see a rare hint of despair. He was on his feet at once and already heading for the door, his heart pounding.

"What's going on?" he demanded. "What's happened?"

"The new man, Billy-Clyde, he got in between that new prize bull of yours and that beast's current love interest. Billy-Clyde's gored pretty bad. I think his leg might even be broke. He needs better care than what he can get here in town. I'd like to get him airlifted over to Fort Worth."

"Do it. Why are you wasting time talking to me? I'll make the arrangements. Where is he now?"

"In the back of the pickup. I thought it would save time. We were real careful moving him, made sure to stabilize his neck and back before we got him off the ground."

Just then Lizzy came rushing into the room. "What is it? I saw the truck outside and all the men hovering around it."

"It's one of the men," Hank said, already reaching for the phone. "He's been gored pretty bad."

Lizzy didn't ask a lot of questions after that. To his astonishment, she began barking orders like the head of a big-city trauma team. Hank made the call for a chopper to fly Billy-Clyde out. By the time he got outside, Lizzy was up in the bed of the truck, blood all over her as she worked to stop the bleeding. Billy-Clyde was passed out cold.

"It's going to be okay," she kept soothing the man anyway. "We'll just get this tourniquet a little tighter." She gave a little nod of satisfaction. "There now, that ought to do it." Looking around, she shouted, "Hank, where the hell's that chopper?"

"On its way," he promised, just as he heard the whir of the medevac unit, then felt the sting of stirred-up dust as it settled into place fifty yards away. The team inside raced for the truck and replaced Lizzy at Billy-Clyde's side. They listened carefully to her report, then went to work on the unconscious man.

Within minutes, Billy-Clyde was loaded into the chopper, ready to be flown toward a Fort Worth trauma center. Pete looked to Hank for permission, then climbed aboard to go with them.

Only after they'd gone and the rest of the men had dispersed to finish herding the cattle onto new grazing land did Hank take a good, long look at Lizzy. She was covered with blood and trembling.

He walked over and touched a finger to her chin. "Hey, you okay?"

Her head bobbed, but she was still shivering as if she'd been doused in creek water again.

"Inside," he said, prodding her toward the front door.

She glanced down at her clothes. "But I'm a mess."

"Doesn't matter," he insisted. Inside, he bellowed for the housekeeper. Mrs. Wyndham took one look at Lizzy and began to cluck.

"Oh, you darling girl, come with me. I'll have you

all cleaned up and changed in no time. Then I'll fix you some soup and some hot tea.''

Lizzy went along with the older woman with surprising docility. Hank watched them go with a sinking sensation in the pit of his stomach. Watching Lizzy take command outside had shaken him more than he'd realized. For the first time, he'd seen exactly what kind of doctor she was going to be—skilled, quick thinking, patient and compassionate.

For some reason, even though it had kept them apart all these years, he'd never taken this medical-school thing seriously. It hadn't seemed to matter that she'd declared it her dream or that she'd gone chasing off after it. He'd always assumed it was just another passing fancy, sort of like that year on the rodeo circuit.

Now he had to confront the fact that Lizzy truly was meant to be a doctor. She had all the quick reflexes and right instincts for it. But there was going to be a long road ahead of her before she could allow the kind of distraction that a home and family would bring. What the hell was he supposed to do all those years? Wait here, hoping that when it was over she'd come back to him? He wasn't sure he was capable of that kind of patience.

He was in his office once again when she came back downstairs, wrapped in one of his robes that was miles too big for her. The sleeves had been rolled up a half-dozen times and the belt looped tightly around her waist with most of the material bloused up over it. Even at that, her bare toes barely peeked out beneath the hem. Hank thought she'd never looked more exhausted or more desirable.

"You did good out there," he said quietly. "How're you feeling?"

"More scared now that it's over." She regarded him wistfully. "Do you suppose that's how every trauma-unit doctor feels? Do you think they just act on instinct and then fall apart afterward?"

"I imagine they do. Otherwise they couldn't do their jobs." He studied her intently. "Is that the kind of doctor you're thinking of being?"

She nodded. "It wasn't at first. Remember how I used to talk about my fancy office and my fancy patients? Then when the idea of studying emergency medicine first took hold, I thought maybe it was just watching too much TV, you know. That I'd gotten the excitement and the satisfaction all wrong." She met his gaze. "But I hadn't. That's exactly how it is." Her excitement faded and was replaced by worry. "Have you heard anything from Fort Worth yet?"

"Pete called a minute ago. Billy-Clyde's in surgery. Pete said the doctors there said your quick thinking gave the boy a fighting chance. They're pretty sure they can save him and his leg."

She smiled wearily. "That's good, then."

Before he could ask what was really on his mind, Mrs. Wyndham bustled in with the promised hot tea, soup and a plate of sandwiches.

"You'll feel better once you've gotten something

into your stomach,'' she told Lizzy. ''All that adrenaline pumping through you takes a toll.''

Hank shot her a look of gratitude.

''Thank you, Mrs. Wyndham,'' Lizzy said. ''You're an angel.''

''Oh, there are some who'd dispute that,'' she said with a wink. ''Including my husband. You call me if you need anything more. I'll have your clothes ready in no time, though I doubt they'll ever be the same again.''

When she was gone, Lizzy tackled the sandwiches with enthusiasm. When the color was back in her cheeks and her hand was steadier, Hank decided to broach the subject that had been tormenting him for the past hour.

''Lizzy, what's going on between you and me?''

She gave him a wry look. ''Don't you know, cowboy?''

''Okay, I suppose the real question is what does it mean to you?''

She swallowed hard and eventually looked away. ''You do ask the tough ones, don't you?''

''I think it's a fair question.''

''I can't deny that, but—''

''But what?''

She regarded him with something that might have been panic in her eyes. ''I'm not sure I have an answer, at least not one you want to hear.''

''Meaning?''

''I needed to find out something when I came back to Los Piños this time. I needed to discover once and for all if there really was anything between us. For too many years, I dismissed what I was feeling as a silly schoolgirl crush. You seemed to take it the same way."

"So this has been an experiment?" he asked, his tone deadly calm.

"No, of course not." She blinked. "I mean, not really. Hank, you know how I've always felt about you. I know you do, even though you spent a lot of time pretending you didn't."

"Okay, yes, I knew."

"Well, I needed to find out if I'd been imagining the chemistry."

"And now that you know you haven't been imagining it? What now?"

She sighed heavily. "I wish I knew."

"Well, that's just great," he said, unable to curb his rising anger. "Terrific. You've sashayed in here and turned my life upside down to satisfy your curiosity and you don't have a clue about what happens next. Fantastic."

She leveled a look straight at him then, a look full of fire and fury. "Do you?" she asked quietly, clearly struggling to restrain her temper. "Do you have a clue?"

"No, dammit. Not after today, I don't."

His response seemed to confuse her. "Today? What does today have to do with it?"

"I saw you as a doctor for the first time. I finally had to face the fact that you're not just playing a game, that you didn't run off to college just to prove some idiotic point to me.''

"Is that what you thought?"

"Yes, dammit."

"And you let me go then because…?"

"Because it was the right thing to do. You were young. You didn't know your own mind, not about me or about school."

"I see. And now that you know different?"

"I don't know," he said miserably. "Nothing I'd meant to do makes sense anymore."

"Nothing you'd meant to do? What does that mean?"

Hank leveled a look straight into her eyes. "It means I was going to ask you to stay," he said quietly. "I was going to ask you to marry me."

Her eyes widened. Her lower lip trembled. "And now you're not?"

Hank met her gaze evenly. "And now I'm not."

Tears spilled over and ran down her cheeks, but Hank couldn't bring himself to go to her. He was too afraid that touching her would only lead to making love. If he held her again, if he felt her body moving beneath his, heard her cries of pleasure, he wasn't sure if he'd be able to let her go the way he knew he must.

Lizzy was in a daze as she left Hank's ranch and drove back to White Pines. Never in her life had she felt more miserable or at a loss. She was the confident one, the one who always knew exactly what she wanted and went about getting it. In fact, that's what she'd done a few days ago. She'd gone after Hank.

Unfortunately, she was also impulsive. She acted without thinking. Now it appeared she was going to have a long time to live with the regrets. Her mother had warned her. She'd told her not to play games, not to start something until she knew precisely how she wanted it to end. Her mother was wrong about one thing, though. She didn't think she'd be bouncing back from pain this deep.

Hank hadn't even given her time to rejoice over his declaration that he'd wanted to marry her before snatching the prospect away from her. There'd been no open door, no chance for her to accept a proposal. In fact, there had never even been a proposal, just the taunting hint that he'd intended to propose.

She'd been tempted to stay and fight him, to try to make him put that offer of marriage on the table, but his expression had been intractable, his tone forbidding. And her mother's warning had finally, too late, begun to echo in her head.

What good would it do to get Hank to propose marriage, when she knew in her heart of hearts that she couldn't say yes, not now, not for a long time? If today's crisis with Billy-Clyde had been a turning point for Hank, it had been one for her, too. It had solidified her resolve to stay the course, to finish med school and become a trauma doctor in some big-city medical center. How could she possibly reconcile the two dreams?

Tears were still tracking down her cheeks when

she got back to White Pines. She slipped inside and tried to sneak quietly back to her room to do some long, hard thinking, but her father met her at the top of the steps.

"I heard what happened over at Hank's place," he said, beaming at her with obvious pride. "Everybody says you saved the day."

"I suppose," she said, trying futilely to wipe away the dampness on her cheeks.

Her father's penetrating gaze never left her face. "Then why the tears?"

"I saved that man's life, but I lost Hank in the process."

"Don't be silly," her father said dismissively. "The man's crazy about you."

"I know that, but he figured something out today. He realized how long it's going to be before we can be together, and it was too long to suit him." She couldn't seem to keep the bitterness and hurt out of her voice.

Her father opened his arms, and Lizzy raced into them. "Oh, Daddy, how can love possibly be this cruel? I finally discover Hank really cares about me, only to lose him."

"You haven't lost him," her father reassured her. "He just needs to get his bearings. He'll wait. When it comes to love, there's no choice."

Lizzy shook her head. "You didn't see his face. It's over. He wants a wife now, not years from now."

Her father chuckled. "That's what he thinks today, but it won't be long before he figures out that the waiting doesn't matter as long as it's for the right woman."

Lizzy wished she could believe that.

"You know I believe it's time we had a little party around here," her father said, his expression thoughtful. "Something grand, that'll have the whole state talking."

"Daddy, you're not up to entertaining."

"Who says I'm not? Maritza will do all the work with whatever help she needs. All I need to do is show up. If I get tired, I can go to my room for a bit of rest. Besides, what's the good of being rich and powerful and old if you can't make things happen when you want them to?"

No one on earth was better at doing just that, Lizzy thought with amusement. Harlan Adams did love to make things happen.

"Who are you thinking of inviting to this party?" she asked.

"Never you mind about that. Go get Maritza and tell her to get up here. If your mama's downstairs, send her up, too."

The gleam in his eyes was a warning. "Daddy, what is going on in that devious mind of yours?"

"Nothing you need to concern yourself with. Why don't you go into town and find yourself a pretty new dress? Something that'll knock Hank's socks off."

"I don't think they have dresses like that in Los Piños."

"Then call your brother. Tell Jordan to have his pilot fly you to Dallas for a shopping spree first thing in the morning. Take your mama along, too. She needs a break from hovering over me.''

Lizzy regarded him doubtfully. ''You won't try sneaking hot-fudge sundaes and pizza while we're gone?''

''Stop worrying about my diet and go.''

It was only after he'd convinced her and after she and her mother were on their way to Dallas first thing the next morning that Lizzy realized he'd never promised her that he'd behave himself.

''Oh, no,'' she muttered. ''Daddy's probably raiding the refrigerator right now.''

Her mother smiled, her expression surprisingly complacent. ''I don't think so.''

''Why not? What do you know that I don't?''

''You know that padlock we've been joking about?''

Lizzy began to laugh. ''You didn't?''

''Oh, but I did. I had one put on the minute your father started making noises about going back downstairs again.''

''Oh, what I wouldn't give to see his expression the first time he sees it.''

''I have that covered, too. I left the camera with Maritza.''

Laughing, Lizzy suddenly felt better than she had since Hank had tossed her right back out of his life before she'd even gotten a toehold in it.

When the laughter died, she saw her mother studying her worriedly.

"When are you going to tell me what prompted your father's latest matchmaking scheme?"

Though she'd suspected as much, hearing her mother say the word made Lizzy very uneasy. "What makes you think it's a matchmaking scheme?" she asked.

"They usually are with him. Besides, I saw the guest list. Half the eligible bachelors in Texas are being invited to this party. I assume they're either meant to produce a new man for you or they're intended to make Hank jealous. So why is your father taking this drastic measure?"

"Actually, Daddy didn't tell me what he had in mind."

"But you know perfectly well what set him off."

Lizzy sighed and filled her mother in on Hank's decision to end their relationship. Instead of the sympathy she'd expected, her mother frowned.

"I see." She regarded Lizzy intently. "Let me ask you something. If Hank were to change his mind and propose, what would you do?"

"Why, of course, I'd..." Her voice trailed off.

Her mother nodded. "I thought so. Lizzy, didn't I tell you to be careful what you wished for? Hank's always worn his feelings for you on his sleeve, but his actions have been decent and honorable. He's let you go your own way. Now you've come waltzing back into town, led him on, slept with him, I imagine, and in a few days you'll head back to Miami, correct?"

"Yes," she admitted in a small voice.

"Do you really need to have him propose for your own ego?" her mother asked with a hint of impatience. "Or do you honestly want to marry the man?"

"It's not about ego," Lizzy said fiercely. "I care about him. I always have."

"Enough to give up med school?"

"Yes," she said impulsively. Then she hung her head and added miserably, "No."

She met her mother's gaze, expecting more condemnation. Instead, this time she found only sympathy.

"Why does it have to be a choice?" Lizzy asked wistfully. "Why can't I have both?"

"Maybe you can, in time, but not right now, not this minute." She smiled. "You always were impatient and just a little greedy."

"Thanks."

"I'm not blaming you for it," her mother explained, reaching over to squeeze her hand. "Your father always gave you everything you ever wanted. You were an unexpected blessing for both of us. Harlan being Harlan, he spoiled you and I didn't do much to stop him, because he enjoyed it so much. Now he's trying to do it again. You want Hank, so he's doing his level best to make sure you get him. Neither one of you seems to be taking into account Hank's feelings."

"He must love me," Lizzy protested. "He almost proposed yesterday. He admitted that much."

"But he changed his mind and, as he sees it, for

a good reason. He didn't want to take medicine away from you by asking you to stay. Maybe this time you're the one who should do the right and noble thing and let him go. Allow him to give you this gift of a career with no distractions or regrets."

Lizzy sighed. "I'm not sure I can. I don't know what I'd do if he went and found someone else. Then I'd live with regrets for the rest of my life."

Her mother reached over and squeezed her hand. "But you'd survive. You're Harlan Adams's daughter and you are every bit as strong as he is. And when it comes to survival, I'm a pretty tough old bird myself. You've got good genes, Lizzy. They'll come through for you."

"But—"

"No, Lizzy, I want you to think about it. If you really love him, think about what's best for Hank."

Lizzy did as her mother asked, which could have turned the shopping expedition into a dismal affair, but she loved clothes a little too much not to get into the spirit of it. With Hank very much on her mind, she picked out a slinky red slip dress beaded with rhinestones for the party.

Then, over her mother's objections, she insisted that her mother pick out something just as sexy for herself. Lizzy just hoped her father's heart was up to the effect of all that bared cleavage.

Not until they were on their way home after dinner in one of their favorite Tex-Mex restaurants did Lizzy allow herself to seriously consider what would happen if she got Hank to change his mind and ask her to marry him, after all.

Could she really give up med school and stay in Los Piños? Would she be content to be a rancher's wife with no career or identity of her own? Hadn't that been the whole point of wanting to be a doctor, to finally make something of herself, something separate from being Harlan Adams's baby daughter? How could she go from being daddy's little girl to being Hank's wife without finding out who she really was along the way?

And then there was medicine itself. She was good at it. She had believed all along that she would be, but yesterday's events had confirmed it. She could be cool in a crisis without losing her sense of compassion. She had always, always wanted to make everyone and everything around her better, from the first injured and abandoned kitten she'd nursed back to health with Dani's help to her parents, whom she'd doctored with chicken soup and cold compresses whenever they caught so much as the sniffles.

At first the idea of taking premed courses had been as impulsive as everything else she'd ever done. By her sophomore year, though, she'd begun to take it seriously as she'd excelled in class after class. Volunteering at the medical center had clinched it. The first time she'd walked through the doors of that bustling facility, it had felt right to her.

Just as right as her feelings for Hank, she thought with a sigh.

She was back full circle. Two dreams, two very

divergent dreams. When she finally fell into a restless sleep on the plane, though, it was Hank's face she saw. And the look of yearning on it was enough to make her weep.

She awoke with a start, her cheeks damp with tears. Letting go was going to be a killer, she thought, glancing over to see her mother sleeping peacefully in the opposite seat. For the first time, she realized exactly how Hank must have felt watching her walk away, letting her leave without saying a word that might have enticed her to stay.

And he was doing it again, keeping that proposal silent so that she could go with an easy conscience and no lingering demands to divide her attentions. She owed him the same kind of freedom.

But she clung to something her father had said. If they were destined to be together, time wouldn't make a difference. Hank would be there when she'd done what she had to do. And if he wasn't, well, she wouldn't be the first woman ever to bury herself in work to hide a broken heart.

Chapter Seven

"What the hell do you mean, you're not coming?" Cody demanded as Hank turned his back and walked away.

Hank sighed and faced the older man. Cody's expression was partly incredulous and partly accusatory. "Which part of that didn't you understand?" he asked, managing somehow to keep his tone even.

"It's a party in Lizzy's honor," Cody protested. "You have to be there."

Clinging stubbornly to his pride and his resolve to let her go once more—this time for good—Hank shook his head. "No law says I have to go."

"What about the fact that you'll be insulting Lizzy and my father if you stay home?"

"That's an exaggeration, and you know it. I doubt

your sister is any more anxious to see me than I am to see her. She's not overjoyed with me at the moment,'' he said in what he considered to be a massive understatement. ''She thinks I'm being bullheaded and downright mean, instead of levelheaded and sensible. Lizzy's not the kind of woman who'd want rejection rubbed in her face.''

He kept his gaze pinned on Cody, who was beginning to look vaguely uncomfortable at being caught in the middle. ''As for your father,'' Hank continued, ''Harlan will get over it. He's described me as antisocial on more than one occasion, when I've turned down his invitations. A family dinner is one thing, but this party is showing all the signs of turning into one of those famous Adams barbecues for the rich and powerful.''

''He's kept the guest list down to a couple of dozen. I swear it. He's really counting on you being there. Besides, the whole reason for this party...'' Cody said, then winced at the clear implication. ''Forget I said that.''

Hank's gaze narrowed. ''Okay, Cody, what is your daddy up to now?'' he asked, as if he didn't know. More matchmaking, most likely. It was Harlan's favorite pastime. Hank wondered, though, if Cody would admit it. He'd always trusted the older man to be straight with him and, when it came to matters of ranching, he was. When it came to family, though, Cody's loyalty was elsewhere.

''Nothing,'' Cody said, though he couldn't meet

Hank's gaze when he said it. "I shouldn't have said anything."

"The words are out now. You can't take them back. If Harlan is up to no good, then that's all the more reason for me to stay as far away from White Pines tonight as possible. Nothing good can come of this, Cody. Trust me. There was only one thing to do under these circumstances, and I've done it."

Cody regarded him slyly. "Lizzy's going back to school in two days. Will you be able to live with yourself if you don't get one last look at her to tide you over till summer?"

"You know, Cody, I would think a big brother would want to keep a man like me as far away from his baby sister as possible."

"Why? No man I know would be a better match for her. You're levelheaded where she's impetuous. She'll be the kind of mother who'll inspire spirited antics. You'll be a terrific, rock-solid father. And you'll give her the moon, if she asks for it. What you're trying to do by staying away from her right now proves that. You're a good man, Hank. The best. Lizzy couldn't do better."

"Thanks for the glowing praise, but right now what Lizzy needs is a mentor in the medical profession, not a husband who'll tie her down."

"Shouldn't you give her the chance to decide that for herself?"

"Not when the deciding will just tear her apart," Hank insisted. "Look, Cody, I know she cares about me. Maybe she even fancies herself in love with me, but that doesn't mean she's ready to get married or even to make the choice."

"Why the hell does it have to be a choice?" Cody retorted impatiently.

"Because Miami's a long way away."

"So what? She doesn't have to stay in Miami. She can come back to Texas and go to medical school here. That'll be close enough to make commuting feasible."

"She chose Miami in the first place just because it was far away. She needs to make her own mark on the world, away from the Adams influence."

"Okay, fine. Jordan has his own damned jet. You can commute to Miami."

The same desperate idea had come to Hank in the middle of the night, but he'd resisted it then and he intended to resist it now. "How many days do you get to take off in ranching? Besides, that's not my idea of marriage," he told Cody. "I doubt it's hers, either. Maybe it would work for a few months, even a year, but Lizzy's years away from setting up a medical practice. Until then, she needs her freedom."

"It doesn't sound to me like it's her freedom that matters. Sounds more like you being set in your ways. What's wrong with being flexible, maybe even a little imaginative, if it gets you what you want?" Cody's gaze narrowed. "Or don't you want Lizzy enough to even try?"

Hank turned away. "You don't know anything about what I feel," he muttered.

"Then tell me," Cody argued, sounding combative. "Tell me why my sister was good enough to sleep with, but not good enough to fight for. And don't try denying the two of you have been sleeping together, because I'm not that dumb. She's not creeping into the house at dawn because you two have been off somewhere picking daises in the moonlight."

Hank turned back slowly. "That's what this is really about, isn't it? It sticks in your craw that she and I slept together, even though you practically dared me to see if I could get her into bed." He reached into his pocket and pulled out a roll of bills. He peeled off some twenties and pushed them toward Cody. "You won. Satisfied?"

"Hell, no, I'm not satisfied," Cody said, shoving aside the money. "Far from it."

"Tough. She's a grown woman, Cody. It was her decision to make."

Cody raked his fingers through his hair. "Dammit, I know that. I don't much like it, but I know it. She'd brain me with a skillet if I said otherwise or if I punched you out the way I'm tempted to."

"Well, then, can't you just leave it be?" Once more he held out the money. "Here, take it. You won it fair and square. Lizzy didn't tell me to take a hike, the way I predicted she would. God knows, we'd probably both be better off if she had."

Cody ignored the hundred dollars and shook his head. "Forget the damned bet." His expression turned sympathetic. "Can I offer a word of advice?"

"Can I stop you?"

"Once upon a time, I took off and hid out, instead of asking the questions I should have asked and demanding straight answers. I'll regret that till the day I die. It cost me a year of my daughter's life, because I didn't even know Melissa was pregnant with Sharon Lynn when I ran."

He gave Hank a beseeching look. "Just come to the party tonight. Talk things through with Lizzy, see if you can't work things out. That's all I ask. What will it be, a couple of hours of your time? Is that so much to ask when your whole future's at stake?"

If that's all it were, no, Hank thought. But it wasn't the time that mattered. It was what seeing Lizzy again was likely to do to his resolve.

"Lizzy and I aren't known for our long-winded, introspective conversations," Hank said.

"You'll be in the midst of a whole throng of people," Cody countered with a wry expression. "There won't be much you can do besides talk."

"I'll think about it," Hank promised. "But don't count on anything."

Cody grinned. "It's not me who's counting on you. It's Daddy and Lizzy. If I were you, I wouldn't want to risk riling either one of them."

Thinking of some of the wicked things Lizzy had done to show her displeasure with him in the past, Hank had to agree. He figured he still had a few hours to weigh that prospect against the danger of seeing Lizzy one last time.

White Pines was crawling with eligible bachelors. Lizzy walked through the downstairs rooms and counted them. There were at least a dozen. Aside from family, it seemed that single males were the only guests. Some were from the state capital. She recognized them as up-and-coming legislators. There were a handful of ranchers from around the state, an oilman pal of Jordan's and a couple of lobbyists from Washington she suspected had been added to the guest list by her cooperative older sister. Jenny had traveled in some powerful circles before she'd decided to come home and teach school.

All in all, her father had outdone himself, she thought with amusement, then sighed.

Only one man was missing, the only one who mattered. Hank couldn't very well be jealous if he never even saw the competition.

"He'll be here," Sharon Lynn promised, arriving at her side and giving her hand a quick squeeze. "I know Daddy had a talk with him this afternoon."

Lizzy frowned. "Cody talked to Hank?"

"Oh, yeah," Sharon Lynn said. "Kyle and I went riding up on the ridge around lunchtime. We could hear Daddy shouting all the way up there."

"Could you hear what they said?" Lizzy asked, even though it was downright embarrassing to be so pitifully eager for information about Hank's state of mind.

"Not really."

Her spirits sank. "Then you don't know if Hank agreed to come tonight or not?"

"No," Sharon Lynn conceded with obvious reluctance.

"Then this whole party is a total waste."

"Not necessarily," Sharon Lynn said. "You could check out the alternatives. Granddaddy has provided a veritable smorgasbord of men for you to choose from. It seems like a shame to waste them. Maybe one of them will be able to take your mind off of Hank."

Lizzy shot her a disgusted look. "Would a total stranger be able to take your mind off Kyle if the two of you were having problems?"

"I suppose not," Sharon Lynn conceded. Her expression brightened. "But if Hank decides to put in an appearance, wouldn't it be better if he walked in and found you engrossed in conversation with some handsome, sexy man, rather than sulking in a corner? Besides, you can't let that dress go to waste. Every male in the room—except Kyle, of course—is practically drooling over you. There's music on the patio. Why not find yourself a partner and go enjoy it?"

Just then, glancing through the French doors, Lizzy could have sworn she'd caught a glimpse of Hank outside in the shadows at the edge of the patio. Her heart lurched. Sharon Lynn's idea began to make a whole lot more sense.

"You know," she said, suddenly more agreeable, "maybe I will go try to persuade one of these men to dance, if you'll have a chat with the band and see if they'll play something nice and slow."

Sharon Lynn regarded her quizzically. "Slow? What are you up to?"

"Never mind. Will you do it?"

"Of course."

Lizzy turned back toward the living room and surveyed the available men. She picked out the tallest, sexiest one there, who also happened to be the oil tycoon. Now, there was a combination that ought to get Hank's attention, as long as he never figured out just how sleazy the man was or how much she disliked him.

She strolled across the room, thoroughly aware of the fact that every male gaze was on her, looked up into Brian Lane's black-as-coal eyes and smiled. "Care to dance?" she asked.

"I'd be honored," he said at once.

He tucked her hand through the crook of his arm and led the way outside. Lizzy didn't miss the triumphant expression on his face as he walked off with the evening's grand prize—her. She would have made him pay for that look, if he hadn't been the perfect choice for the little game she had in mind to torment Hank.

Brian Lane was just over thirty and heir to a family fortune. A lot of women would have keeled over under the heat of those dark, mysterious, hooded looks he'd perfected. Lizzy had met him at Jordan's on several occasions in the past. She knew how quickly that heated gaze could turn coldly assessing. For all his polite social skills and oodles of money and privilege, Brian Lane was not a very nice man, which was why she'd always declined his invitations to dinner.

But he was exactly the predatory sort of male that drove other men into possessive rages. Even her cool-as-a-cucumber big brother seemed to get a little nervous when Brian began paying a little too much attention to her sister-in-law.

On the patio with the music suddenly and oh-so-conveniently turning slow, he drew Lizzy into his arms just a little too tightly. He would have paid for that, too, had it not suited her purposes. She wondered, as he moved to the music's provocative rhythm, if he had any idea that instead of being swept away by the feel of him, she was busily searching the shadows for a glimpse of another man. She doubted it. Brian was not prone to self-doubts.

"I always knew one day you'd come around," he murmured against her ear.

Lizzy stumbled. "Excuse me?"

"You've been playing hard-to-get since the first time we met at your brother's house," he said. "I figured it couldn't last too much longer. There's always been a chemistry between us. I've sensed it. I know you must have, too."

If he'd been serious, Lizzy would have been nervous, but she'd heard him use the exact same line too many times. She found it laughable but, wisely, she fought that particular reaction. For the moment, she needed him to play the role of ardent suitor.

Brian seemed to take her silence for assent, because he increased the pressure on her back, forcing her even more tightly against him. She felt the first twinge of panic when she realized that he was fully aroused. The second twinge came when he tried to waltz her into the shadows, away from the other dancers.

Well, hell, Lizzy thought. She had not started this game to cause a scene, but Brian was rapidly changing the rules. Just when she was about to chill his amorous intentions with a well-placed and savage kick, the gap between them suddenly widened and Hank moved smoothly in between. No man had ever cut in on another with such tactical precision or such an expression of grim determination.

Hank gave the other man a smile edged with ice. "Thanks for looking after the lady," Hank said in a chilly tone that wasn't nearly as grateful as the words implied. "But I'm here now."

Brian opened his mouth to protest, but Hank's steady, lethal gaze seemed to change his mind. He glanced at Lizzy instead.

"We'll catch up with each other another time."

"I doubt it," Hank said, making it clear that the other man shouldn't even try.

Brian shrugged finally and walked away, but it was clear from his expression that Hank had just made an enemy. Even so, Lizzy felt relief shimmer through her. Not that she intended to let Hank catch so much as a glimmer of it. She intended to see him suffer for the heartache he'd put her through the past few days.

"Was that some sort of macho ritual I just witnessed?'' she inquired lightly, as if she found the study of such behavior fascinating in a purely academic way.

Hank gave her a wry look. "That was me saving you from getting mauled by that creep. Who the hell was he anyway?"

"A business associate of Jordan's."

"Jordan ought to choose his friends more carefully."

"I didn't say they were friends," she began, then shrugged. "Never mind. Did you even stop to consider that maybe I wanted to get mauled?"

His response to that was a hard, silent stare. Lizzy winced and gave up the game. "Okay, maybe I am grateful that you turned up when you did."

He shook his head. "Something tells me you were counting on it. What I can't figure is how you even knew I was around. I haven't even set foot on the patio until now, much less been inside."

"I guess I must have a sixth sense about it when you're around." She grinned at him. "Or maybe you're just not as good at sneaking around and hiding in the bushes as you thought you were."

His cheeks flamed with color. "You saw me?"

"Sure did."

"Then that whole scene was deliberately staged for my benefit?"

"I never said that."

"You didn't have to." He regarded her with amusement. "Give it up, Lizzy. You were trying to make me jealous. That's what this whole charade of a party is about. Your daddy didn't even make a pretense of it being anything else. There's not another single woman here. All those men were meant to be prospective competition for me.''

"Okay," she said cheerfully. "Since it worked, I suppose I can admit it. Not that I planned it, of course. This was Daddy's doing.''

"I'm sure," he agreed. Then he added softly, "It doesn't change anything.''

She refused to accept that. "Of course it does,'' she insisted. "It proves that you can't just turn your back on me, after all.''

"I wasn't turning my back on you," he said wearily. "I was trying to let you go." He studied her intently. "That's still the plan, Lizzy. What just happened doesn't change that.''

He tucked a finger under her chin and forced her head up. "If you'll tell the truth, you wouldn't want it any other way, either. You have to go back, darlin'. You know you do.''

Tears welled up, but she fought them. "Can't we at least have the next couple of days, then? Please." She waited through the longest silence of her life, then added, "That's as much begging as I'm ever going to do, Hank Robbins, so what is it? Yes or no?''

She saw the torment on his face and the indecision. Finally he sighed. "Yes," he whispered against her cheek. "We'll steal every second that we've got left.''

"Can we leave, then?''

"You're the guest of honor," he noted. "It wouldn't be polite."

She'd never regretted her ingrained sense of duty more. "I suppose."

Hank grinned. "Now that the party's served its purpose, you're bored with it, aren't you?"

"I was bored with it before. Now that you're here, I suppose I can make the best of it." She looked up into his eyes. "Hold me a little tighter, cowboy, and let's pretend we're at your place, all alone."

"Oh, no, you don't," he protested, keeping her at arm's length. "Cody's already put me on notice where you're concerned. If I try that right here in plain view, I'll have a whole passel of shotguns aimed straight at my belly. You and I would be standing at an altar before we could blink."

"Would that be so bad?" Lizzy asked wistfully.

Hank stroked his knuckles down her cheek. "You know that's not the way you want it to happen. You don't want the decision taken out of your hands."

"Maybe I do," she said with a touch of defiance.

"A marriage begun like that between the two of us wouldn't last a month. You'd start resenting me and the situation in the blink of an eye. You know you would."

If she was being honest, Lizzy couldn't deny it. She wondered, though, about Hank. "What about you? Would you resent me, too?"

He took a long time answering, long enough for her heart to climb into her throat and tears to threaten.

"*Resentment* is the wrong word. I'd just be torn apart knowing how badly you wanted something and that I'd played a role in preventing you from getting it. Starting a marriage with regrets is no way to make it last."

"You're being noble again, aren't you?"

He grinned at her. "It is a curse, trying to be honorable around you. You make it mighty hard, Mary Elizabeth Adams. Mighty hard."

Lizzy's spirits brightened. "Then you are tempted, at least?"

"Be patient, darlin'. We ought to be able to sneak away from here by midnight. Then I'll show you just how tempting I find you."

"Promise?"

"Cross my heart."

Lizzy sighed contentedly and tucked her head on Hank's shoulder, where she could indulge herself in the feel and scent of him. "Then you know what I'm tempted to do?" she murmured.

"What's that?"

She looked up and met his gaze. "I am very tempted to slip inside and start moving every clock in the place forward a couple of hours."

Hank chuckled. "You'd do it, too, wouldn't you?"

"Oh, yes," she agreed. "But Daddy has gone to a lot of trouble to make tonight happen. I suppose I should make sure he gets his money's worth." She broke free of his embrace. Still holding on to his hand, she led him inside.

"Where are we going?" Hank asked, wondering if she intended to make good on her threat to start moving time forward.

"To show Daddy that his scheming worked one more time."

Hank stopped, forcing her to halt as well. "Bad idea, darlin'."

"Why?"

"Because you'll get his hopes up, and you and I both know that we're not together for good."

"We're not?"

"No," he said emphatically.

"What, then?" she asked, as her heart began to thud dully.

"We're just saying a long goodbye."

Chapter Eight

The goodbye took forty-eight hours and it was the most bittersweet experience of Hank's life.

Once he and Lizzy had slipped away from White Pines and Harlan's smug glances, they had driven to his ranch, raced each other for the front door, stripping away clothes as they'd run. They had made love the first time in an urgent frenzy, right in the foyer, with Lizzy's back braced against the wall, her legs wrapped around Hank's waist.

Later there had been sweet, slow loving in his bed, lingering caresses just because they couldn't stop touching and frantic, uninhibited sex so memorable that just the thought of it could make Hank's blood heat.

For once Lizzy had stayed through the night,

awakening in his arms with a sleepy smile and wicked suggestions that had touched off the passion all over again.

This morning, though, her imminent departure had cast a pall over them. They sat at his kitchen table with eggs and toast getting cold on their plates and coffee adding to the acid churning in Hank's stomach.

Finally, he forced his gaze to the clock above the stove. "It's about time, darlin'."

She shot him a shattered look. "Already?"

"Afraid so."

Her lower lip trembled. "I'm not sure I can do it."

"You don't have a choice."

Her chin tilted stubbornly. "Of course I do."

Hank grinned at the flaring of Adams defiance. "Not really."

She regarded him with an unwavering look, then sighed. "I suppose not. I just didn't know it was going to hurt this much." She searched his face. "But you did, didn't you?"

Hank nodded, because he suddenly couldn't speak around the huge lump that was forming in his throat.

"It's worse this time," she whispered. "Much worse."

Again he nodded. "Because now we know for sure. We're good together, Lizzy. Really good. That ought to be the only thing that matters, but we both know it's not."

"We could make it the only thing," she said with grim determination.

"No, we couldn't," he told her, reaching for her hand. "We've been over this a million times, and I've been over it a million more in my head. If I thought there was another way, I'd hold on to you and never let you go, but there's not. You have to go back, and I need to stay right here. I wanted my own place my whole life. I've spent the last few years turning this old wreck into a halfway decent ranching operation. I can't turn my back on it now."

"I know," she admitted. "But I'll only be gone a few weeks and then we'll have the whole summer. We'll just have to concentrate on that."

Obviously, she'd meant it as consolation, but Hank wasn't sure he could bear the thought of summer's torment, having her with him again, only to say goodbye...again. But telling her that now would only make today more difficult, and he wasn't sure he could bear to see any more hurt in her eyes.

"Just a few weeks," he echoed, and left it at that.

"Will you go with me to the airport in Dallas?" she asked. "Jordan's flying me over."

"Are you sure you wouldn't rather say goodbye here, in private?"

"I would, but I also want to hold on to every possible second we can be together."

He thought of all the work that needed doing around the ranch, all the duties he'd already left to his foreman during Lizzy's visit home. What was one more day, though? Pete could manage. He'd be glad to, in fact. The way the man seized responsibility and followed through was one of the reasons he and Hank got along so well. He'd been pushed out of his last job by an employer who thought he'd gotten too old for it. He'd been hell-bent ever since on proving to Hank that he was still up to managing a ranch.

"I'll go with you," he said. "Just let me give Pete a call and tell him I'll be gone for most of the day. Or would you rather I drive you over to White Pines first, so you can have time to say your goodbyes there?"

"That's probably best. I still have a bit of packing to do, too. You can drop me off, then come back around noon. Does that work for you?"

He grinned. "If it works for you, it works for me."

After he'd left her at White Pines, though, he began to imagine turning this into a routine that could last for years yet. Goodbye after goodbye, none of them getting any easier. It would never work, not even with the promise of forever at the end. Neither he nor Lizzy was known for patience. It was the single trait they had in common and the worst one they could have shared under the circumstances.

And yet when he thought about the alternative—never seeing Lizzy again—he couldn't imagine that, either. The very thought made his gut churn. Surely no two people had ever been caught in a more agonizing catch-22, destined to be miserable whatever choice they made.

He remembered what Lizzy had said earlier: summer was right around the corner. Maybe that was soon enough to make the choice, after all. In the meantime, he imagined his long-distance telephone bills were going to be astronomical.

"Daddy, I have to go. Hank's waiting and Jordan's probably already at the airport grumbling about me being late," Lizzy said, giving her father a fierce hug.

"Let 'em wait," he grumbled. "You're my darlin' girl, and I want to know how you're doing before I let you get away from here." He searched her face. "Since you've spent the past couple of days with Hank, does that mean what I think it means? Are you two working things out?"

"We're trying, Daddy."

"Don't make the man wait around too long, Lizzy. No man can put his life on hold forever. You shouldn't, either, for that matter."

"Are you telling me I should give up medicine?"

"I can't tell you that. It's your decision. I'm just saying you need to be sure you have your priorities in order. If Hank's the man you want, then grab on to the love you two have and don't let go. Not for anything." He grinned. "You know, I hear they have a couple of pretty good med schools right up the road a piece. You could choose one closer to home."

Lizzy nodded. "I know."

"And fall would be the perfect time to make a change," he added.

"Daddy, you can't just switch med schools at the

drop of a hat," she protested. "Admissions are getting more and more difficult."

"You just say the word, and I'll make it happen," he vowed.

Her mother walked in on them then. "Harlan, are you throwing your weight around again?"

He grinned at his wife. "Threatening to," he admitted. "If it'll get my girl what she wants."

"You know, if you indulge her every whim, she'll never bother figuring out what it is she really wants enough to fight for it. You made the boys stand up for what they wanted and you did okay by them, didn't you?"

"Except for Eric," he said quietly, making a rare reference to the son who'd died in an accident on Luke's ranch. "I tried to make a rancher of him, when he wanted to teach. I like to think I learned from that." He sighed. "I can't help remembering what that cost me, Janet. If it's in my power to make one of my own happy, then I want to do it."

"And your precious Lizzy has you twisted around her little finger," her mother said.

Lizzy grinned and kissed his cheek. "Which is what makes you the most incredible father in the universe, but Mom could be right this time. I have to figure out what I want and then I have to be the one to make it happen."

Her father held up his hands. "Okay, okay, I can't fight the two of you. Just promise me you'll let me know if you want any help."

"It's a deal," Lizzy said. She turned and hugged her mother. "Take care of him, you hear."

"She always does," her father said, already slipping an arm around her mother's waist.

When they walked outside, they found Hank waiting beside his pickup, Lizzy's bags already loaded in the back.

"All set?" he asked.

Lizzy forced a smile. "All set."

She gave her parents one last hug, then climbed into the truck. Hank started the engine, then glanced over.

"You okay?"

She gave him a halfhearted smile. "Sure."

He pulled away from the house, watching in the rearview mirror as Harlan and Janet waved goodbye until the truck made the turn in the lane that took it out of sight. He braked then and reached over to brush the tears from Lizzy's cheeks.

"He'll be here when you get home," he promised, even though he had to know it was up to fate, not him.

Lizzy lifted her tear-streaked face to meet his gaze. "What if—?"

"No, darlin', don't even go there. Imagining the worst doesn't help anybody. You saw for yourself that Harlan was getting stronger every day."

"That's what he claimed, anyway."

"He was out of bed the day after you got home," he reminded her. "He danced with your mother at your party. And he just walked down the front steps to say goodbye without even breathing hard. By the time you get back, he'll be out riding again and you two can go chasing over White Pines land the way you used to. I bet he'll even be interrupting our picnics down by the creek.''

Lizzy paled at the very idea. ''Lordy, I hope not. The shock might give him another heart attack.''

''Oh, I think he has a pretty good idea what you and I have been up to.''

''Knowing it and stumbling in on it are two very different things,'' she retorted. ''I don't think even Harlan Adams is that broad-minded.''

''In that case, no more private picnics by the creek for us,'' Hank taunted.

''There's always nap-time, I suppose,'' Lizzy speculated thoughtfully. ''Even before the heart attack, Daddy did like his little afternoon catnaps.''

''Or maybe we can just put some bells on his horse's bridle.''

''He might wonder about that,'' she said, grinning at last.

''See, there. I made you smile.''

''You always could. That's how we met, remember?''

''How could I forget? Whatever happened to that boy who made you cry that day?''

''I believe he ended up in jail for cattle rustling,'' she said, unable to keep the note of satisfaction out of her voice.

''A fitting end for the jerk,'' Hank declared.

"What was it he did to you? You never did tell me that."

Lizzy winced. "Okay, it wasn't all that awful, now that I think back on it, but I was sixteen at the time. Every slight was a mortal wound back then."

"What was it he did?" Hank repeated.

"You're really going to make me say it, aren't you?"

He nodded. "I really am. Something tells me I'm going to enjoy the heck out of whatever you're trying so hard not to say."

"Okay, okay. He refused to carry my tray in the cafeteria. Are you satisfied? It was my first public humiliation."

Hank barely managed to hide the grin tugging at his lips. "Devastating, I'm sure."

"Well, it was. All the other boys were doing it for me. He was the only one who wouldn't."

"Which naturally made him the most attractive," Hank said.

"Of course." Lizzy moaned. "Jeez, I was such an idiot."

"You were a teenage girl," he corrected.

"Maybe idiocy and hormones do go together," she said. "Anyway, you were wonderful. You didn't treat me as if I was sixteen and my problem was nonsense. You listened and then you teased me and you made me smile, just like today. I've never forgotten that."

"Neither have I," he said quietly, glancing over

at her as he pulled into the small airport where Jordan was waiting for them. "Neither have I."

"Hank, I—"

She never got to finish the thought because Justin yanked open the door of the pickup, his expression disgruntled. "It's about time you got here. We were supposed to take off a half hour ago."

Lizzy stared at him. "What are you doing here?"

"I'm catching a lift to Dallas, too. I'm checking out the police academy there."

"And Jordan is actually flying you over there?" she asked, incredulous. Her brother's willing participation in Justin's defection from the oil business was astounding. Jordan didn't like losing. It was another of those infamous Adams traits.

Justin shrugged. "He's resigned to it. My hunch is he's hoping I'll flunk out and put an end to what he refers to as 'this utter nonsense.'"

"Now, that sounds more like him," Lizzy said. "Stick to your guns, though, Justin. No pun intended."

Hank groaned. "Hey, Justin, how about giving me a hand with these bags? Lizzy has never grasped the concept of packing light."

"It's not all clothes," she protested. "I have some medical texts in there, and they weigh a ton."

"And how many of those books did you crack while you were home?" Justin teased. "Hank, is that what the two of you were doing over at your place? Studying?"

"Exactly," Lizzy retorted, regarding Hank boldly.

"I had a little trouble with my anatomy class. Hank was making sure I got it right."

"I'll bet," Justin retorted. "My hunch is there was no textbook involved."

Just then Jordan came around the side of the hangar and glared at all of them. "Is anybody planning to fly to Dallas today?"

"Sorry," Hank said. "Saying goodbye to Harlan took a little longer than we anticipated."

Jordan's frown eased as he searched Lizzy's face. "He's okay?"

"He's fine. I just got a little crazy when it came time to walk away."

Her brother nodded sympathetically. "I've had that trouble myself from time to time lately. Now that everybody's here, though, let's get this show on the road. I don't like the looks of that storm that's brewing to the west. I checked with the tower and we're cleared to go, but the window of opportunity won't last forever."

Lizzy cast a nervous look toward the western horizon. It looked perfectly clear to her, but she knew the unpredictable Texas weather well enough to know that it could change in a heartbeat. "Jordan, are you sure?"

"We'll be fine, if we quit wasting time," he assured her.

"Then let's do it," Hank said.

They climbed aboard Jordan's corporate jet and settled into their seats. Justin, who'd been flying since his sixteenth birthday, took the copilot's seat, which left Lizzy alone with Hank in the main cabin.

The takeoff was smooth, the trip uneventful except for an occasional pocket of turbulence that flipped her stomach upside down. Each time it happened, she reached for Hank's hand and clung to it.

"Lizzy, darlin', your brother is an experienced pilot, and Justin's no slouch himself. We're in good hands."

"I know that," she agreed. "Just in case, though, there's something I want to say to you."

Hank seemed to guess her intention because he reached over and pressed a silencing finger to her lips. "Don't."

"I have to," she insisted. "I have to say it just once."

"Lizzy—"

"I love you, Hank. No matter what happens, I want you to remember that. I love you."

A muscle in his jaw twitched, and his whole body tensed as if she'd slapped him. Eventually, though, he sighed. "I love you, too, darlin'. I truly do."

"Then we'll find some way to make this work," Lizzy promised. "I know we will."

Hank gave her a rueful smile. "I wish I shared your confidence."

She forced her brightest grin in an attempt to overcome his doubts—and her own. "You would if you'd been born an Adams. We believe we can make anything happen. That's Daddy's grandest legacy to us."

"So I've noticed," he said dryly. "There are powerful international leaders who aren't so sure they can sway things to their liking."

"But you've seen it," she persisted. "You have to know we always get what we want."

"Sometimes I've seen you bend what you want to suit what you get."

"That's the pragmatic side of our nature. It comes in handy on those rare occasions when things don't work out quite the way we anticipated."

"Turning lemons into lemonade," Hank suggested.

"Precisely."

"Well, all I can say is, I hope we're not about to drown in the stuff."

"Hank Robbins, you are such a pessimist."

"I'm a realist, and I'd say one of us needs to be."

"Realism is depressing," Lizzy countered. "Want to know what I see for our future?"

Hank grinned. "Sure. Go ahead and entertain me."

"I see me graduating from medical school. Then I see me serving my internship and my residency."

"So far, this seems to be all about you. Where am I while you're making medical history?"

She grinned. "Waiting for me at home like a dutiful husband, maybe getting dinner on the table while I study."

"You do have a vivid imagination, I'll give you that. Who's running my ranch?"

"You are, of course, with Pete's help. You're

making the decisions and taking care of the long-range planning, buying the cattle for breeding and studying the futures market for beef. Pete's doing the hands-on work.'' She regarded Hank hopefully. "He can handle it. You know he can."

"He can," Hank agreed. "But he shouldn't have to. He's a foreman. I'd be a lousy owner if I left all the hard work to him."

"Texas is loaded with rich absentee ranchers."

"I'm not rich and I have no intention of being an absentee anything."

"You haven't even considered the idea," Lizzy protested. "Couldn't you at least give it some thought?"

"I don't have to think about it," Hank said. "It's impossible."

"In other words, if any compromising is going to be done, I'm the one who's going to have to do it. My career automatically has to take a back seat to yours."

Hank scowled. "I never said that."

"You didn't have to say it."

"Do you really want to waste what little time we have left arguing about this ridiculous idea of yours?"

"So, now I'm ridiculous?" she practically shouted.

"I didn't say you were ridiculous, dammit. I said the idea was absurd."

"It's the same thing."

Justin stuck his head into the main cabin. "Hey, you two, do you need a referee back here?"

"No," they shouted in unison, glaring at each other.

"Well, at least you agree on something," Justin said, grinning.

"You are not going to practice negotiating domestic disputes on us," Lizzy muttered.

"Okay, then. Have it your way," Justin said agreeably. "Call me if you change your mind. By the way, Dad says he's thinking of circling the airport until the two of you resolve this. Keep in mind that this plane only holds so much fuel."

"Very amusing," Lizzy retorted. "Now go away."

After he'd gone, she drew in a deep breath and faced Hank. He was staring out the window, his expression enigmatic.

"Hank?"

"Yes," he replied without turning.

"I'm sorry."

He sighed and faced her. "I'm sorry, too, darlin'."

"If I come over there, will you kiss me?"

A slow grin spread across his face. "Only if you lock the cockpit door."

Lizzy was on her feet in a heartbeat. She locked the door, then hurled herself into Hank's waiting arms, only to have the intercom switch on and Jordan advise them they were making their descent into the Dallas–Fort Worth airport.

"Get back into your seat, Mary Elizabeth, and fasten that seat belt," her brother said, his voice laced with amusement. "I am not operating a motel room at twenty thousand feet."

Hank picked up the phone that allowed the passengers to communicate with the pilot. "Too bad, Jordan, because I would pay you a whole lot of money for a couple more uninterrupted hours up here."

"I don't want to hear that," Jordan retorted. "I definitely do not want to hear that."

Without the benefit of a phone of her own, Lizzy simply raised her voice. "You are such a prude, Jordan."

"I think my wife might disagree, little sister."

"And I don't want to hear about *that*," Justin chimed in. "Can't we just get this plane on the ground, please? Lizzy's flight's in an hour, anyway."

Jordan chuckled. "Happy to oblige, son, but something tells me the odds on her making that flight are not real good."

Lizzy's gaze locked with Hank's. "There is a later flight, you know. I checked before we left home."

"Jordan's not going to want to wait around forever," he said with regret.

Apparently, he'd forgotten to disconnect the phone to the cockpit, because Jordan responded, "That weather system's moved in behind us. We're grounded till morning. You're on your own, Hank. I'm sure you can find a way to spend the time."

"Yes," Hank agreed, never taking his gaze from Lizzy's face, "I imagine I can."

Chapter Nine

It was morning before Lizzy finally caught a flight back to Miami. Hank watched her board the plane, then turned and walked away. If he'd stayed, there was a very good chance he'd have bought a ticket and gone to Miami with her. That was the kind of impulsive thing Lizzy might do, but not him. He'd always prided himself on being sensible. Somehow, though, when he got around Lizzy, he lost his head.

When he met Jordan an hour later, Lizzy's brother regarded him sympathetically. "Saying goodbye doesn't get any easier," he said. "I tried it with Kelly for a while. I commuted back and forth to Houston, certain that my company headquarters had to be there. She was just as determined never to set foot in that city again. She'd hated it when she'd lived there with her ex-husband and she'd vowed never to go back. All she ever wanted was to live on her family's ranch in Los Piños."

It was a sentiment Hank could share, and obviously Jordan saw the connection.

"She turned that ranch around single-handedly," he said with obvious pride. "Did you know that?"

"I'd heard the story," Hank said. He studied Jordan's expression, then asked in a low voice, "Did you ever wish she'd fail?"

Jordan's eyes widened with surprise. "Is that what you're hoping for? That Lizzy will fail at med school?"

Hank sighed. "No, not really, not when she has her heart set on it, but it would make things a hell of a lot easier."

"Easy's not always for the best."

"Another one of those Adams lessons on life?"

"No, just an observation. Daddy's always gone about making life easy for Lizzy," he said without rancor. "It's understandable, her being the youngest and his first girl, if you don't count Jenny, who was already half-grown when Daddy married her mama. Lizzy needs some challenges. She needs to know she can handle them on her own."

His expression turned thoughtful. "The same thing was true with all of us, in one way or another. With Luke and Cody and me, Daddy put every obstacle he could in our way to make us fight for what we wanted. It worked. We're all stronger men because of it. He hasn't done the same with Lizzy. In her case, I think it's going to be up to you to show her what she's made of.''

"And you think I'm up to the challenge?" Hank inquired.

"Oh, I know you are. So does Daddy. But until you've figured that out for yourself, what we think doesn't matter a tinker's damn."

Hank laughed despite himself. "One of these days, I'm going to have to ask the women you guys married if the Adams men were worth the trouble they caused."

"What answer you'll get probably depends on which day you ask. We're not always easy, but Harlan Adams set a high standard for all of us. You'll be getting the best there is, if you can work things out with Lizzy."

If, Hank thought. For a little, old two-letter word, it had the power to bring a strong man to his knees.

"So, what happened with the hunky rancher?" Kelsey demanded the minute Lizzy reached the small apartment they shared near the University of Miami med-school campus.

Lizzy's hands stilled on the rumpled clothes she was plucking out of her suitcase. "What makes you think anything happened?"

"Well, if I didn't know it before, your reaction just now confirmed it." Kelsey settled down cross-legged in the middle of Lizzy's bed. "Spill it. Did you see Hank? More importantly, did you sleep with him? Is that why you were a day late getting back, because you couldn't bear to leave him?''

Lizzy chuckled. ''You know, Kelsey, your imagination is entirely too vivid. I think it's time for you to get a social life of your own. Or maybe to give up medicine and write one of those romance novels you're always reading in your spare time.''

''No time,'' Kelsey replied, waving off the suggestion. ''Besides, observing yours is entertainment enough.''

''Sorry. You're about to be cut off.''

Kelsey blinked. ''Cut off? How come? You aren't moving out, are you?''

''No, of course not. Just putting my social life here on ice.''

''I knew it,'' her roommate shouted jubilantly. ''You did sleep with him.''

Before Lizzy could reply, the phone rang. Grateful for the interruption, she grabbed it. ''Hello.''

''Hey, darlin', miss me yet?''

''Heavens, no,'' she lied. ''I've barely had time to think, much less miss you.'' She caught Kelsey observing her with fascination.

''Hold on a sec, will you?'' she asked Hank.

''Sure.''

She scowled at her roommate. ''Kelsey, privacy, please.''

''Only if you will swear to fill me in on what went on in Texas,'' she said, still not budging from the bed.

"How about if I swear to kill you if you don't scoot right this second?"

Kelsey grinned. "That works, too." As she exited the room, she shouted over her shoulder, "Hey, Hank, come see us."

Lizzy grimaced and picked up the phone. "You heard?"

"Indeed. Who was that?"

"My roommate, who has developed a sudden fascination with cowboys. Think I ought to get her one of her own?"

"Possibly. Is she gorgeous?"

"Do you think I'd tell you if she were?"

"Hmm. I'm picturing five-ten, long blond hair and the face of an angel."

"And I'm picturing you dead."

Hank chuckled. "I do love it when you get all possessive on me."

"Must be a guy thing. Women hate jealous men."

"Really? Didn't seem that way when you were kissing up to old Brian at your daddy's party."

"That was different."

"I'd love to hear how."

"It was necessary, part of a larger plan, so to speak."

"And the larger plan was to what? Make me declare my intentions?"

"Something like that."

"So if I mention that I went to Garden City today, that would be okay?"

Lizzy's heart slowed. "You went where?"

"To Garden City," he said, his tone all innocence. "Right after Jordan and I got back."

"I suppose you went to explain why you hadn't been around for the past week or so."

"Something like that."

"Was she forgiving?"

"Always is," he said.

"Then she's dumb as a post," Lizzy countered. "The two of you would never last. You don't need a quiet, accepting woman in your life. You need one who's going to rip your heart out if you stray."

"And that would be you?"

"That would definitely be me," she agreed.

"I'll try and remember that."

"You'd better," she said in a dire tone. "Exactly how much time did you spend in Garden City, anyway?"

"Long enough."

"Long enough to do what?" she demanded.

"What I went there for." He sighed. "Oh, darlin', I do miss you. I wish you were here right this second."

"Then that visit to Garden City must not have been nearly as exciting as the flight to Dallas. What would you do if I were right there beside you?"

"Use your imagination."

"Oh, no. I want you to spell it out for me."

"Now, on the phone?"

"Yep." She settled back against the pillows on her bed and let Hank's low, sexy voice roll over her. It was that voice as much as the wicked suggestions he made that made her pulse race and raised goose bumps.

"No, stop," she whispered in a choked voice when the torment got to be too much.

"Lizzy? What's wrong?"

"Nothing. It's just that I didn't realize how lonely it would make me feel to want you so much and know you're so far away."

"Oh, baby, I know. Believe me, I know."

"Will you call me later?"

"What time? Do you have classes this afternoon?"

"A couple, but I'll be back here by suppertime. Then I'll be studying."

"I'll call you right before I go to bed, then, to say good-night. Okay?"

At least his would be the last voice she heard before falling asleep, Lizzy thought. It would be almost like having him in bed beside her.

"Later, then," she said. "I love you."

Only after she'd put the receiver back in the cradle did she realize that Hank hadn't said he loved her, too. She'd thought she had opened the door to that on the plane, but maybe Hank had only felt obliged to say the words with her staring him in the face. Maybe he'd never meant them at all.

"No," she told herself sternly.

She wasn't going to do this, she vowed. She wasn't going to succumb to doubts on her very first day away from him. If she couldn't trust Hank, if she couldn't believe in their love, then they were doomed and she refused to accept that outcome. They had started something wonderful back in Texas, and she was going to hang on to that with everything she had.

Hank was feeling restless when he got off the phone. The house seemed empty, even though he could hear Mrs. Wyndham bustling around in the kitchen. He had to get out and do something, maybe remind himself why this ranch was so all-fired important to him.

He headed for the barn and saddled his big bay gelding, Uncle Sid, named for a relative of its previous owner who'd apparently been every bit as fractious as the horse. Even now, years later, Uncle Sid danced skittishly as Hank saddled him.

Maybe a hard ride was what he and the horse needed. He could check out some of the downed fence lines Pete had told him about. The foreman suspected they'd been cut through deliberately, possibly by someone hoping the cattle would be put back in that distant pasture and then stray.

It could have been mischief or the first step toward thievery. At the moment, it was a distraction from missing Lizzy, and that was all that mattered.

He urged the horse into a full gallop, hoping the wind would chase away the erotic images he'd meant to stir only for Lizzy. Unfortunately, the game had backfired. It had left him hot and aching, as well.

He hadn't stopped to consider how late in the day it was. Dusk began to fall as he reached the distant fence. He slowed his horse over the uneven terrain. Uncle Sid whinnied nervously.

"It's okay, fella. There's nobody around but us."

Uncle Sid seemed to disagree, fighting the bit in his mouth. It had been a long time since the old bay had acted up this way. Hank gazed through the gathering darkness, searching for movement in the shadows, but seeing nothing. Even so, he was glad he'd thought to bring his gun along.

As he neared the fence line, he spotted the downed barbed wire and broken posts. One could have been split by lightning, but a whole row of them? Not likely. He was about to climb down for a closer look when Uncle Sid turned skittish and danced away from the fence.

At a whizzing sound, the horse shied. Hank clung to the saddle horn, but there was no soothing the frightened animal. Uncle Sid bucked and bolted, heaving the unsuspecting Hank into the air. One foot caught in the stirrup as he fell. He hit the ground with a jarring thud, only to be dragged within inches of pounding hooves as Uncle Sid raced back toward home.

He managed one hoarse shout, but the horse was beyond hearing. Then Hank bounced hard. His head hit something, most likely a rock or fallen tree limb, and the world went black.

Fortunately, the same thud that had knocked him unconscious also jarred his foot free of the stirrup. He was left lying in the dust, alone in a pitch-black night.

He had no idea how long it was before he began to come to. He knew only that the sky was filled with stars and his head ached worse than the worst hangover he'd ever had. He tried to move, then moaned at the pain that shot through him. Bad idea, he concluded and lay still.

The air began to cool as the night deepened. Hank shivered and tried to keep himself awake. Wasn't that the right thing to do with a concussion? If only Lizzy were here, he thought. She would know. She would make the blinding pain go away.

"Supposed to talk to her," he murmured, trying to struggle to his feet once again, only to fall back to the ground with a moan.

He fought sleep, fought to cling to consciousness, only to lose the battle. When he came to again, it was to the sound of hoofbeats and shouts.

"Over here," Cody called out to someone. "He's on the ground over here."

Hank forced his eyes open, only to snap them shut again as the glare of Cody's flashlight fixed on his face.

"Turn that damned thing off," he grumbled.

"Can't be hurt too bad if you're complaining about the rescue," Cody noted.

"How'd you know to come looking for me?" Hank asked.

"You can thank Lizzy for that," Cody said. "When you hadn't called her by midnight, she called me, fussing up a storm with some tale about you being near death."

"Where'd she come up with that?"

"I wondered the same thing. She claimed the only way you wouldn't have called her was if you were half-dead. She insisted I come over to check on you."

Cody grinned. "I tried to explain that a grown man might resent another man checking on him in the middle of the night." He shrugged. "You know Lizzy. She threatened to call Daddy if I wouldn't agree to do it. I couldn't very well let her send him out into the night on a wild-goose chase."

"How'd you know to look out here?"

"A little guesswork and an understanding of your compulsive nature. Your horse was outside the barn with its saddle still on and covered with dust, looking like he'd been ridden hard. I roused Pete, and he told me about the fence. We added up two and two and here we are."

He probed Hank's leg, checking for broken bones. Hank winced but didn't cry out. Cody gave a nod of satisfaction. "Bruised but not broke, I'd say."

"I'd prefer that guess had come from your sister."

"You mean you'd prefer it was Lizzy's hands doing the poking and prodding, more than likely. She's got a gentler touch than I have, no doubt."

"No doubt," Hank agreed with heartfelt sincerity. "Can we get out of here now? I would really like to spend what's left of the night in my own bed."

"Afraid that's out of the question," Cody said. "Lizzy insisted we take you to the hospital to get you checked out. We can go to the one in Garden

City. It can't handle major trauma, but something tells me you just need an X ray and maybe a patch or two on a couple of cuts."

"I'm not going to the damned hospital," Hank protested.

"Are you going to be the one to tell Lizzy you refused?" Cody asked. "Because I'm sure as hell not. She'll be on the next plane back from Miami. It'll disrupt her studies and she'll have to take this last quarter over, prolonging her med-school career. I was under the impression you wanted her to finish sooner rather than later."

Hank groaned. "All right, all right. I'll go to the hospital, but I am not checking in. Is that understood?"

"Understood," Cody agreed, then amended, "unless the doc says it's vital to your well-being."

"You are nothing but a damned bully, Cody Adams."

"And I'm a saint, compared to my baby sister. Be glad she's in Miami."

Hank tried to be glad about that. He really did, but a part of him longed to have her there making a fuss over him. It would have irritated the daylights out of him—no doubt about that—but he still wished she were the one doing the fussing.

By the time he'd been X-rayed and bandaged and poked and prodded by the medical experts in Garden City, it was past daybreak. Cody brought him home, filled Mrs. Wyndham in on the doc's instructions and left Hank to grumble about being confined to bed.

Fortunately, when his temper was about to flare into full-fledged rebellion, the phone rang.

"Yes," he barked.

"Ah, I gather the patient is awake and chipper," Lizzy taunted.

Hank's temper cooled at once. "Hey, darlin'."

"Cody told me what happened. Are you really okay?"

"I'm fine. I gather I owe you for calling out the troops last night."

"I knew something was wrong when you didn't call."

"And it never once occurred to you to think I might have forgotten?"

She was silent for a full minute. "Actually, at first that is exactly what I thought. I was ticked about it, too. Then I decided you'd just decided not to call and that made me even madder, so I called you to give you a piece of my mind. I kept calling for an hour. When you didn't answer, I called Cody."

"I could have been in Garden City, you know."

"Not a chance," she insisted.

"Why are you so sure of that?"

"Because I know you. You do not have a death wish."

Hank would have laughed, but it hurt too much. He smiled instead, glad that she couldn't see it.

"You are really okay, aren't you?" she asked, sounding plaintive.

"Bumps and bruises, nothing serious."

"And a concussion," Lizzy corrected. "Cody told me that."

"Cody has a big mouth."

"I wish I were there. I'll bet I could keep you from falling asleep."

"I'll bet you could, too," he agreed.

"Maybe I should come home," she suggested.

"No way. You stay right where you are and finish the school year. I don't want to see you lose time because of me."

"I won't be able to concentrate anyway."

"Who are you kidding? I heard you finished an English exam once with a tornado bearing down on the building," Hank teased.

"I did not. It was a little old thunderstorm. I was twelve, anyway. I thought I was invincible."

"But all the other kids were cowering under their desks," he reminded her. He had always loved that story about Lizzy. To him it epitomized her grit and daring. He glanced at the clock beside his bed. "Shouldn't you be on your way to class now?"

"It's only a ten-minute walk. I'll run," she said. "Tell me about the fence you went out to check on. Cody says it looks like it was deliberately downed."

"Could be," Hank agreed.

"Why?"

"Somebody after cattle, I imagine. Or just up to no good."

"The same somebody who let that bull loose that gored Billy-Clyde?"

Hank hadn't made the connection before, but he

should have. He muttered a harsh oath under his breath.

"Hank? Do you think it's possible the two incidents are linked?"

"It's possible," he said grimly. "I don't know why the thought didn't occur to me before. There was no reason for that bull to be on the loose that day."

"You never said what spooked Uncle Sid last night."

"I'm not sure, to tell the truth." He remembered the whizzing sound just before the horse bolted. It could have been a gunshot with the bullet coming close enough to terrify the horse or even nick him. "I've got to go, darlin', and you need to get to your class. We'll talk later, okay?"

"Hank," Lizzy protested, but he already had the receiver halfway to the cradle.

He hobbled out of bed and yanked on his jeans. The movements were painful, and his head throbbed like a son of a gun, but by heaven he was going to the barn. If that had been a bullet flying last night, it very well could have nicked Uncle Sid and the evidence would be unmistakable. If he found so much as a scratch on that horse's hide, there was going to be hell to pay.

Chapter Ten

Two weeks after Hank's accident, Lizzy stared at the positive home-pregnancy test she was holding in her hand. For a week, she had blamed her low energy level and queasiness on stress, but the missed period had been a symptom she couldn't ignore. It had taken an act of courage to walk into a pharmacy and buy the pregnancy test. Now she could only stare at the results in dismay.

It couldn't be, she told herself even as she held the clear evidence right in front of her eyes. She couldn't be pregnant.

Well, of course she *could be,* she corrected. No birth-control method was one hundred percent foolproof. They'd used two, which should have improved the odds, but even then…

Had there been once when Hank had failed to reach for a condom or even once when she'd failed to take her birth-control pill? Or were they just two of the unlucky few whose birth control simply failed?

She wanted desperately to blame that little blue dot on Hank, but there had been two of them in his bed and they'd both been responsible, at least every single time she could recall.

But all it took was once, she reminded herself, one tiny slip. She didn't need a medical textbook to tell her that.

At least she finally knew why she'd been feeling so lousy for the past few days. She hadn't really needed a textbook for that, either. She'd guessed what the nausea, light-headedness and exhaustion added up to. She just hadn't wanted to believe it, because it had the potential to change everything.

She grasped the edge of the sink as a wave of dizziness washed over her. Pregnant. She repeated the word several times in her head, trying to force acceptance. Instead, there was only shock.

A baby. Hank's baby. At any other time, she would have been thrilled beyond belief to be carrying his child. A few years from now, this would be the happiest news she could receive, but now? Now it had her reeling, cursing the impossible timing that threatened years of dreams and planning. This forced their hand in a way she'd never imagined.

How was Hank going to react? she wondered. Would he be stunned? As dismayed as she was? She doubted the latter. Her own father had said that Hank was ready to marry and settle down. Hank himself had broken off with her when he'd finally accepted how long their separation was destined to be. That silly party and the game played with Brian Lane to make him jealous were the only reasons they were still together at all.

Still, even though he was all too determined not to stand in the way of her career, he would be ecstatic at this turn of events. He would book the church and invite the guests before she could blink.

Hank would want her back in Texas permanently. She could just hear him railing on and on until she gave in. He would demand they get married at once and her medical career be damned. Even though he understood her passion for medicine, even though he knew that this was something she had to do, he would fight her for the sake of their child. And as strong as she was under normal conditions, she might not have the strength for this particular battle.

She walked back into her room in a daze and sank onto the bed, huddled against the pillows. When the phone rang, she ignored it. It would be Hank, and she couldn't talk to him right now. He would guess something was wrong and pester her until she told him. Then it would be all too easy to get swept up in the plans he was bound to make.

She listened to the beep on the answering machine, then heard his voice.

"Hey, darlin', just wanted to say hi. I thought you'd be back from class by now, but I guess you're running late. You'd better not be off on a hot date. Call me when you get in."

The machine chirped another beep, then went silent. Tears tracked down Lizzy's cheeks. She knew she had to tell Hank about the baby. It was not the kind of news she would ever consider keeping from him. But she wasn't ready just yet.

She wasn't ready to make the choices that would have to be made. She wasn't ready to deal with all the pressure, from Hank and everyone else, to come home, get married and settle down as a rancher's wife. She'd been a cowgirl all her life and she'd loved it, but she'd wanted more. So much more.

The only thing she was prepared to admit was that she loved the baby's father and that she would love this baby they'd conceived, no matter how it turned her life upside down.

Kelsey rapped on her door then and called out. "Lizzy, I know you're in there. Is something wrong?"

"I'm fine," she insisted.

"You don't sound fine. Can I come in?"

"Not now," she said, even as the door pushed opened and Kelsey entered anyway, her brow knit with concern.

"You didn't pick up the phone when Hank called."

"How did you know it was Hank?" Lizzy grumbled. "Listening at the keyhole?"

"Ever since he got hurt, he calls at the exact same time every night so you won't worry."

"Oh."

"Why didn't you talk to him? Did you two have a fight?"

"No."

Kelsey clearly wasn't about to let it go. When it came to persistence, she could be an honorary Adams. She plunked herself down beside Lizzy and studied her intently. "Tears, too, I see. Come on, Lizzy, if something's wrong, maybe I can help."

"You can't help," Lizzy told her. "No one can."

With no answers forthcoming from the source, Kelsey glanced around the room. Almost at once her gaze fell on the box the pregnancy test had come in.

"Oh, dear," she murmured, glancing into Lizzy's eyes. "That's it, isn't it? You're pregnant?"

Lizzy nodded miserably.

"The baby's Hank's, isn't it?"

"Of course it's Hank's," Lizzy said indignantly.

"Then that's a good thing, yes?"

"Normally, yes, but now?" she asked plaintively.

"Will he be upset?"

"Never."

"Then this is about you and school and your career," Kelsey guessed.

"Of course."

"Then I don't see the problem. Your family's rich as sin, you can hire a zillion nannies if you have to. You can make it work."

Lizzy regarded her friend ruefully. "I don't think Hank's going to go for nannies raising our baby."

"Well, he'll just have to change his way of thinking. You bend a little, he bends a little and it works. That's all there is to it.''

"Thank you, Ann Landers." She sighed. "Hank is not the kind of man who's inclined to bend, even a little."

Kelsey regarded her with a steady look. "What's the alternative? Would you end the pregnancy?"

"Never," Lizzy said, a protective hand on her stomach. "Not in a million years."

"Will you keep the baby a secret?"

That wasn't even a consideration. Even if she didn't believe fiercely in Hank's right to know, she had too many family members who could spill the beans...and would, if they thought it in her best interests. There would be no secrets kept for long in Los Piños, not from Hank or anyone else.

"No," Lizzy said.

"Then I think you'd better have something very specific in mind by the time you tell him or you'll get swept up in his plans."

Lizzy gave her friend a wry look. "Which is exactly why I didn't answer the phone."

Kelsey nodded. "Of course." She was silent for several minutes before she asked, "Any ideas?"

Lizzy sighed. "Unfortunately, not a one."

All she knew for sure was that when she did come up with a plan, it had better be a doozy.

"Have you talked to Lizzy lately?" Cody asked when Hank ran into him in town.

"Not for a couple of days, actually," Hank admitted. "I've had trouble catching up with her. What about you?"

"No. Nobody at White Pines has been able to reach her, either. You don't suppose something's wrong?"

Hank had wondered that very thing. "What could be wrong?"

Cody shook his head. "I don't have any idea. If it were up to me, I'd just chalk it up to the fact that she's Lizzy and that she's a female, but Daddy doesn't seem inclined to let it go at that. He's getting all worked up over it."

"Maybe you ought to leave a message for her to that effect. You know she'd never intentionally worry Harlan."

Cody nodded. "Good idea. I'll try it later. If you get through to her, let me know what you find out."

Hank nodded. "You do the same."

Up until now, Hank had been making excuses for not being able to reach Lizzy. Surely if something were truly wrong, he would feel it, just as she had known there was a problem the night he hadn't called her as scheduled. The fact that she wasn't talking to anyone at White Pines, either, made him very uneasy.

He walked into Dolan's and approached Sharon Lynn. "Hey, sweetheart, mind if I use your phone? I'll put it on my credit card."

"Help yourself, but if you're going to call Lizzy, don't bother," she said. "I just tried and got that blasted answering machine again. She can't possibly be in classes or off studying at the library twenty-four hours a day.''

Hank's stomach knotted. "Then you're worried, too?"

She nodded. "This isn't like her. Lizzy always stays in touch, especially now."

"Because of her daddy."

"Exactly. She never goes more than a day or two without calling. And I'm trying to reach her about the wedding. If I don't get her soon, I'm going to see to it her maid-of-honor dress is chartreuse with lots and lots of ruffles. She'll hate that."

"Damn," Hank muttered. "What about her roommate? Does she have a separate phone line?"

Sharon Lynn's expression brightened. "Of course. Why didn't I think of that? I'll call Kelsey right this second."

"Mind if I wait while you do?"

Sharon Lynn grinned. "Any chance I could stop you?"

Hank shrugged. "Doubtful," he said, sliding onto a stool at the counter as she picked up the phone and began to dial. When she'd gotten the roommate's number from Miami information, she dialed again.

"Hello, Kelsey? This is Sharon Lynn Adams, Lizzy's niece."

To his thorough frustration, Hank couldn't hear what the other woman said. He glanced around to see if he could spot another extension of the store phone and saw one behind the pharmacist's counter. He went over and grabbed it up just in time to hear

Kelsey stammering some sort of an excuse about Lizzy being really busy lately.

"Is anything wrong?" she asked Sharon Lynn worriedly. "Nothing's happened to her father, has it?"

"No, but he's worried sick about her. So are the rest of us."

"Wait," Kelsey said. "She just walked in the door. I'll get her for you."

Hank heard her explaining to Lizzy that Sharon Lynn was on the phone. Lizzy's reply was too low for him to catch, but a moment later she came on the line.

"Sharon Lynn? Is everything all right at home?"

"Other than all of us being worried sick about you, yes. What's going on? Nobody's been able to reach you for days."

"School's tough," she said unconvincingly. "I'm spending all my time studying."

"You're sure that's all it is?" Sharon Lynn asked, her skepticism plain.

"Of course," Lizzy said. "What else could it be?"

"I'm glad to hear it. Wait a sec, there's someone else here who'd like to say hi." She gestured toward Hank.

"Hey, darlin'," he said quietly.

"Hank?"

It sounded to him as if her voice trembled. "Yep, it's me. I just stopped by Dolan's, and Sharon Lynn and I decided to try to track you down."

"I see."

Her dull response, everything about the conversation sounded wrong to Hank. "Lizzy, what's really up with you? And don't try that bull about being too busy studying to call."

"It's the truth. I told you I wasn't doing all that well in my classes before I left for spring break. I'm trying to catch up now."

"And I've got a patch of swamp in the Everglades I'd like to sell you for an amusement park."

"You don't have to be sarcastic."

"I think I do. Come on, Lizzy, talk to me. What's going on?"

"Nothing."

Hank's frustration was escalating by the second. "Is it me? Are you having second thoughts about us?"

She sighed. "No, that's not it."

"But there is something?" he persisted, determined to drag it out of her.

"Hank, I've really got to go."

That distant, cool note was back in her voice, and it was the last straw. "Go where?" he demanded. "You just walked in the damned door."

"And I don't need you yelling at me," she shouted right back. "We'll talk later."

"When?" he asked, but he was talking to air. The phone clicked off in his ear.

Incredulous, he turned to stare at Sharon Lynn. "She hung up on me."

"Something is definitely wrong," Sharon Lynn

said. "I heard it in her voice. Now the only question is which one of us is going to go to Miami to find out what it is."

Hank thought of the problems that had been cropping up at his ranch, then dismissed them. Pete would stay on top of things. Lizzy was more important.

"I'll leave first thing tomorrow," he said.

"Jordan could fly you down. Maybe someone from the family should go along anyway."

"No," Hank said adamantly. "Something tells me that whatever's wrong has to do with me. If she intends to dump me, I don't want witnesses."

"Lizzy wouldn't dump you," Sharon Lynn protested. "Not in a million years."

Hank thought of the conversation they'd just had. "Well, she just gave a darned good imitation of it."

Even after she'd hung up on Hank, Lizzy stood frozen in the middle of Kelsey's room.

"Big mistake," she murmured to herself.

Kelsey stared at her. "What was a big mistake?"

"Hanging up on Hank."

"Why?"

"Because he's probably already making reservations to come here."

"I know you probably don't want to hear this, but maybe that's for the best. The two of you can talk about this face-to-face. If you don't settle it, you're going to wind up flunking out of school anyway. You haven't been able to concentrate worth a darn ever since you found out you were pregnant.''

Lizzy sank down on the side of Kelsey's bed. ''But I still don't have a plan.''

Kelsey reached for paper and pen. ''Then we'll make a list of all the options. We are both very smart women, which is why they admitted us to this med school. I'm sure if we brainstorm, we'll be able to come up with something ingenious.''

Two hours later, they had crossed off everything except ''marry Hank'' and ''flee to Paris.''

''Okay, we know I am not going to Paris,'' Lizzy said, ''tempting though it might be. That leaves us with one choice, to marry Hank and settle down in Los Piños.''

''You say it as if it's a death sentence.''

''It is a death sentence for my medical career.''

''You don't have a medical career, at least not yet.''

Lizzy scowled at her roommate. ''Thanks for pointing that out.''

''I'm just trying to be realistic.''

''I could do with a heavy dose of fantasy about now,'' Lizzy said plaintively.

''No, you couldn't. You need real, logical alternatives. I still don't see what's so wrong with transferring back to Texas to attend school. You could take off the next year to have the baby, then start back the following fall.''

''I could,'' Lizzy agreed. ''It's just that I'm terrified that once I drop out, I'll never go back again.

Hank is very distracting. Add in a baby, and I'm liable to turn into housewife of the year.''

"Then that will tell you something, won't it? It'll tell you that you don't want this career as badly as you think you do.''

"But I do,'' Lizzy protested. "I need to have my own identity and I love medicine. I'm good at it.''

"Then you'll find a way to make it happen,'' Kelsey said with confidence. "Now, go and get some sleep. You don't want Hank to walk in the door and take one look at you and conclude you're deathly ill.''

"I look that bad?''

"Worse, actually, but it's nothing a little sleep and some of those outrageously expensive cosmetics of yours can't fix right up.''

Lizzy started toward her own room on the other side of the apartment, then turned back. "What if I'm wrong? What if he doesn't come, after all?''

Kelsey grinned. "I don't think you need to worry about that. From everything you've told me about Hank Robbins, he is not the kind of man to take a brush-off lightly. He'll be here. If not tomorrow, then the next day.''

And once he heard her news, Hurricane Andrew would seem like a mild weather system compared to the tornado Hank was likely to stir up.

Chapter Eleven

All of Hank's worst fears had been confirmed in that brief conversation with Lizzy. There was something terribly wrong. For a few days now, their talks had been tense, and more often than not she ended them after little more than a hello and goodbye. It had been disconcerting, but not disturbing.

Then she had stopped taking his calls altogether. When she'd cut him off that afternoon practically in midsentence, he'd recognized that their relationship was in serious trouble. What was driving him nuts was why.

One minute, everything between them had been fine. The next minute, she'd been avoiding him and, just as inexplicably, everyone else back home. The latter made no sense at all, not if her problem was with him.

A less self-confident man simply might have interpreted her behavior as a kiss-off and taken the hint, but it only strengthened Hank's resolve to get to the bottom of the change in her. He wasn't walking away from what they'd found together, not without a battle.

He was pretty sure he knew what had happened. With a little space and perspective, she'd gotten scared of the deep emotions they'd discovered. Hell, the feelings had scared the living daylights out of him, too. Their passion was more powerful than anything he'd ever experienced before. But it wasn't something he intended to turn his back on. Instead, he took the first flight he could get to Miami the following morning.

When he got to her apartment building, which was only a few minutes from the airport in the heart of the University of Miami's Jackson Memorial Hospital medical complex, a young, pumped-up security guard stopped him before he could get to the elevator.

"Who are you here to see, sir?" he inquired politely, his accent surprisingly Southern, rather than the Cuban Hank had anticipated with his dark hair and olive complexion.

"Mary Elizabeth Adams," Hank told him. "I know the apartment number. I'll go on up."

"Sorry. Guests need to be announced," he said in a tone meant to cut off options. "Besides, Ms. Adams left for class a few minutes ago."

Hank couldn't hide his frustration. "What about her roommate? Is she there?"

"Nope, they have the same class this morning."

Frustration turned to irritation. This kid couldn't be a day over nineteen, but his uniform gave him a certain amount of smug self-confidence. Hank was not good with authority figures. He never had been, and to make it worse, this one was still wet behind the ears.

"You're awfully damned familiar with their schedule," he accused. "Why is that?"

The guard never even flinched under Hank's penetrating glare. "I make it a point to get to know the tenants. It makes the atmosphere friendly and my job easier. I can spot trouble faster."

Hank still didn't like it, but he backed down at the sensible explanation. "I see."

"You could wait here," the guard suggested. "But I doubt either one of them will be back before lunchtime. I could show you where to go for a cup of coffee."

"Maybe you could show me where their classes are instead. I'll go wait outside the building."

"I'd feel better if you just came back and waited here."

Hank was getting really irritated with the man's zealous protection of Lizzy, but then he thought about it. If the guard wouldn't let him near her, then he wouldn't let anyone else cause her harm, either. And in a city like Miami, that could be a very good thing indeed.

He smiled. "Look, I'm sorry. It's just that I've flown up here from Texas and I'm anxious to see her. I didn't mean to take it out on you. I know you're just doing your job. So where is this coffee you mentioned?"

The young man beamed at him. "You have your choice," he said, and began gesturing toward a variety of hospital cafeterias and fast-food restaurants in the area. "If you've been cooped up in a plane, you might want to take a walk over to Bascom-Palmer. That's the eye institute a couple of blocks east of here. They have a real nice cafeteria. You can get a decent cup of coffee and some nice blueberry muffins there, or there's a deli in the main complex that has those fancy flavored coffees, if you're into that sort of thing."

Hank nodded. "Old-fashioned coffee, black, will do just fine. And you're right, the walk will do me good. Can I bring you anything when I come back?"

The guard's expression brightened. "If you wouldn't mind, one of those muffins would be great. I used to work in that building and I surely do miss them."

"You've got it," Hank said, and took off in the direction the guard had indicated. He walked through the bustling complex with growing astonishment. It was like a small city with the tiny, original, pink stucco Miami City Hospital building—called the Alamo for reasons he couldn't fathom—tucked in its center, surrounded by towering new structures. Patients in hospital gowns and robes, visitors and employees lingered on benches in the parklike setting around it.

He tried to envision Lizzy as a part of this and couldn't. She'd grown up in the wide-open spaces of Texas. Wouldn't all of this concrete make her as claustrophobic as it was making him? He was about to walk between two buildings when he noticed the sign on one declaring it the Rosenstiel Building, headquarters of the University of Miami School of Medicine. Instead of moving on, he found a bench nearby and settled down to watch the door. The protective security guard would just have to wait for his muffin.

With the constant ebb and flow of people around him and the mix of conversations in Spanish and English with an occasional bit of what was probably Creole thrown in, it was impossible to tell when classes might have let out. He kept his gaze glued to the door of the med-school building.

It was the better part of an hour before he finally spotted Lizzy. She was with a group of students, her expression animated as they debated something or other. Her beautiful, long hair was twisted into some kind of a neat knot on top of her head, and she was dressed in linen slacks and a silk blouse. The look was casual, but clearly dressier than what she usually wore on the ranch. She looked—he searched for a word—professional, he decided.

He knew the precise instant when she spotted him. Shock registered for just a moment in the depths of her eyes. Hank stood, but waited where he was, allowing her time to excuse herself from her circle of friends, rather than forcing introductions.

It seemed to take forever before she finally broke free and came his way, her expression wary rather than welcoming.

"This is a surprise," she said.

Her unenthusiastic tone suggested it was anything but a surprise. Hank had the feeling she'd been expecting him and that her guard was already up. "Really?" he asked. "I would have thought you'd know that hanging up on me was practically an invitation for this visit."

Guilt flickered in her eyes. "Okay, yes. I'm sorry about that. You could have just called back, though. You didn't have to fly all the way over here."

"I thought I did."

"Why?"

"I missed you," he said, and let it go at that for now.

"I wish you'd let me know you were coming."

"Why? So you could tell me not to?"

She winced, then lifted her chin. "Yes, as a matter of fact, that is exactly what I would have told you. I have enough pressure with my classes right now. I can't afford any distractions."

Hank bit back an angry retort. With effort, he kept his tone mild. "Is that all I am, a distraction?"

"Here, yes," she said.

He regarded her evenly, trying to guess what was really going on in her head. Her words were deliberately designed to push him away, but there was something in her eyes that contradicted it, a soft yearning perhaps.

Or was that only wishful thinking on his part? Was she so different here? Had this massive medical complex swallowed up his carefree, joyous Lizzy and replaced her with this studious, solemn woman? He was damned well going to find his Lizzy before he left.

"Can you spare time for lunch at least?"

"I only have an hour."

"Fine. I understand there's a good cafeteria at the eye institute. Shall we go there?"

She nodded at once, looking relieved. Had she been afraid he would suggest her apartment? Was she so terribly frightened of being alone with him? Why? Was it because she was not nearly as immune to him as she wanted to be?

If he'd thought she would relax during lunch, he was mistaken. She left the table in a rush twice and came back looking paler each time. Something was terribly wrong, and with a dawning sense of shock, he had a feeling he knew what it was. He recognized all the symptoms, including the mood swings she'd evidenced in their brief conversations. If his guess was correct, he wanted her to be the one to tell him. Confronting her with a demand to know if she was pregnant with his baby would only put her on the defensive and set them up for a royal battle.

"Lizzy," he said quietly. "Talk to me."

She made a feeble attempt to pretend she had no idea what he wanted to know. She quickly switched to small talk, asking about everyone back home, going through the list of relatives one by one.

"You just talked to Sharon Lynn yesterday," he reminded her. "I suspect you probably checked in with your father last night, since she told you he was worrying about you. I know you know all of the news. Let's get back to what's going on with you."

"Classes, studying," she replied evasively. "You know what it's like."

"Actually, I don't. I've been in ranching all my life. I never went after a college degree." All of which she knew, he thought as he watched her face. There was a hint of panic now that she knew the safest topics were exhausted. He reached across the table and grasped her hand in his. Her skin was like ice. Obviously, his plan to draw her out wasn't working. He might as well be direct and damn the consequences.

"Okay, darlin', let's get straight to it. Tell me about the baby," he finally said.

With that, she burst into tears and ran from the cafeteria and the building, straight into a tropical downpour. Hank caught up with her on the sidewalk down the block. He put his hand gently on her shoulder. She turned, her eyes filled with tears, and then she was in his arms, sobbing against his chest.

"I didn't mean for it to happen."

"Well, of course you didn't," he said, surprised that she would believe he might think that of her. Then he realized what she really meant. He looked her straight in the eyes. "Neither did I."

She sighed. "I know."

"Do you really?"

"Yes, it's just that…" She shrugged.

"It's just that you're feeling overwhelmed and scared and mad."

She frowned. "I hate it that you can read my mind."

"No, you don't. It saves time."

Her chin jutted up defiantly. "I can't marry you, you know."

"We'll talk about it," he said.

"I can't."

"I said we'll talk about it. Right now, I'm getting you back to your place. You're soaking wet. You're dead on your feet, and it's not even the middle of the day."

"What about my classes?"

"You can skip them for once. Have you been getting any sleep at all?"

"Enough for me," she insisted, then gave a rueful smile. "Not enough for the baby, apparently."

That afternoon while Lizzy slept, Hank grappled with their dilemma. The woman he loved was going to have his baby. She was also determined not to let that little predicament change her plans for her career. He'd seen that famous Adams stubbornness in her eyes and in the lift of her chin. She'd practically dared him to insist on marriage.

Hank knew better. Not even God Almighty could force an Adams to do something he or she wasn't ready to do. He was going to have to be patient. He was going to have to wear her down or think of a compromise. Not to marriage, of course. He wouldn't compromise on that. He might be willing to adjust the timetable a bit, maybe find some alternatives to the traditional living arrangements, at least for the time being.

Unfortunately, as good as he was at reading Lizzy, there wasn't nearly time enough to come up with answers to all the arguments she was bound to have against their future. His flight back to Texas was booked for that evening. Once again they were going to be separated, only this time he was going to be the one doing the leaving unless he made some quick arrangements so he could stay.

He called Pete first.

"No problems here," the foreman assured him.

"No more downed fence lines? No weird accidents?"

"Nothing. It was probably just kids, nothing to worry about. You stay right where you are as long as you need to. The boys and me will keep this place humming."

"Thanks, Pete. I'll check in with you."

After talking to Pete, he called the airlines and changed his flight. He scheduled it for the next day, then thought about it and made it for the end of the week. He'd never convince Lizzy to do what needed to be done in a matter of hours. It was going to take days, and that was only if she was in an amenable frame of mind.

He was pacing in the living room when her roommate came back. The girl, who appeared years younger than Lizzy though she had to be nearly the same age, blinked at him from behind her thick glasses. He recognized her as one of the students who'd been with Lizzy earlier.

"Oh, my," she murmured. "You must be Hank."

"I am. And you're Kelsey."

"Yes."

He gestured toward a chair. "Have a seat, Kelsey. I think it's time you and I got to know each other."

Kelsey's gaze snapped toward Lizzy's room. "I'm not so sure that…"

"You and Lizzy are friends, right? And Lizzy and I are—" he searched for the right word "—close."

Kelsey watched him silently.

"Which means we both have her best interests at heart," he concluded.

"Sure," she conceded.

"I imagine the two of you have talked about the baby," he said, watching her face intently. Surprise registered at once in her eyes.

"You know?"

"I know."

She regarded him with indignation then. "What are you going to do about it?"

"I'm going to marry her," he said at once. "But that's easier said than done. I need your help."

"What can I do?" She shrugged. "You know how Lizzy is. Once she makes up her mind, it's not so easy to change it."

"No kidding," Hank said with heartfelt agreement. "But you can tell me what she's been thinking since she found out about the baby. If I'm going to come up with a solution, I need to know where her head is."

"Mixed up," Kelsey said succinctly.

Hank nodded. "Scared, too, I'll bet."

Kelsey seemed shocked by the very idea of that. "Lizzy scared? No way."

"Not even of losing out on medical school?"

"Okay, yes," she conceded. "You're right about that. She's really determined to finish."

"Here, I suppose?"

"Actually, I suggested she transfer back to a school closer to home, but she does seem to be set on finishing here. It's like some weird point of honor with her. I have no idea why. I mean, this school is good, but so are lots of others."

Hank nodded. It was every bit as bad as he'd expected. He had his work cut out for him. "Thanks, Kelsey. You've been a big help."

"Really?"

"Really."

She stood up and backed away nervously. "Well, if you're sure everything's okay here, I think I'll just head off to the library to study."

"You don't need to leave on my account."

"Yes, I do," she said firmly, then grinned. "If you and Lizzy are going to discuss this, there won't be much peace and quiet around here for studying."

Hank grinned back, liking her better and better. "You do have a point."

"Will you be here when I get back?"

He glanced toward Lizzy's room and sighed. "That's my plan," he said. "It remains to be seen what Lizzy has in mind. She may decide to kick me out."

Kelsey regarded him doubtfully. "You don't look like the kind of man who'd be kicked out so easily."

"You're right about that. I am a very stubborn guy."

Kelsey gave a little nod of satisfaction. "Then I'd say the two of you are a perfect match."

After Kelsey had gone, Hank settled back in the easy chair by the window and stared out toward the medical complex. Life-and-death decisions were made there every minute, more than likely. People got well. Some died. And babies were born.

As he thought of the latter, an idea came to him. When Lizzy awoke and walked into the living room a few minutes later, he had the beginnings of a plan.

"Come here, darlin'."

She walked toward him, her gaze every bit as wary as when she'd first seen him earlier. "What?"

He beckoned her into his lap. She hesitated for a moment, then settled into his arms with a sigh. When he held her like this, it was almost possible to believe that everything was going to be all right.

"How're you feeling now?" he asked.

"Better."

"Do you feel up to going for a walk?"

She stared at him in surprise. "A walk? Where?"

"You'll see," he said. "Are you game?"

She studied him intently, then finally nodded. "I'll get my purse."

Hank held her still. "Not just yet. First, we have the little matter of a proper greeting."

She regarded him speculatively. "Proper?"

He chuckled. "Okay. Improper." He smoothed the tendrils of hair away from her face, then ran his thumb over her lower lip. Her gaze heated. By the time he tucked his hand behind her head and drew her toward him, he could see the wanting in her eyes. His own body hummed with anticipation.

It seemed like forever since he'd held her like this, even longer since he'd tasted her. Once he'd started, he couldn't seem to stop. The kiss set off a blazing fire that could only lead to one thing.

But even as he scooped her up and headed toward her room, he had second thoughts. Gazing into her face, he asked hesitantly, "Is this okay?"

She nodded. "Yes. It's okay."

"It won't hurt the baby?"

"No. Believe me, I've already read most of the prenatal books in the med-school library."

Still, he was ever so gentle as he placed her on the bed and lay down beside her. He held back the urgency of his own desires to caress slowly and more and more intimately, until she was pleading with him for more.

"Not yet," he whispered, taking his time removing her clothes, trailing his fingers along sensitive flesh, watching the trail of goose bumps left in his wake.

When she was naked, he studied her, looking for changes in her body, running his hand over her belly, trying to envision his child growing inside her. The image was beyond him, but oh, how he wanted to see her body swollen with his baby. And he would. She wouldn't keep him away from sharing in this miracle.

"Hank?"

He blinked and gazed at her. "Yes?"

"Why such a fierce expression?" she asked, smoothing her hand across his brow.

"Just thinking about the months ahead," he said.

"Don't," she pleaded. "Be here, be with me now."

The longing in her voice reached him and forced aside thoughts of the future. He was here with her now and he could use this incredible connection to keep her with him always.

"I'm here," he whispered, his voice husky.

He rose over her and, with his gaze locked with hers, he entered her slowly, sinking into slick, moist heat that was life's most powerful lure. Ever conscious of the baby, he moved with care until Lizzy stole that option from him with a thrust of her hips that demanded more.

Control slipped away, and he was lost to sensation and need—his and hers. Their skin beaded with perspiration, making the glide of each caress exquisite torture. Their movements became more and more frenzied, until at last Lizzy cried out with release. As her body pulsed around him, he, too, exploded with a climax more shattering than any he'd ever felt before.

With a last, shuddering sigh, he rolled onto his back, carrying her with him. He gazed into her eyes. "You okay?"

"I will be when I can breathe again," she said. She grinned. "You?"

"I'm not the one who's pregnant."

For the first time since the topic had first come up, wonder spread across her face. "I am, aren't I? I am actually going to have a baby."

"You're not scared, are you?"

"Of being pregnant? No."

"Just of the changes it will bring," he guessed.

She nodded and tears sprang to her eyes. "It complicates everything."

"And yet you never once considered ending the pregnancy, did you?"

"Never," she said fiercely.

"Because it's ours," he told her, his hand once again resting across her still-flat tummy. "A part of you and me."

"Yes."

"Then we can work out the rest," he promised her.

"I don't see how."

"One day at a time," he told her. "When life throws us a curve, that's the best any of us can do."

"You're not angry?"

"No way. I want this baby, every bit as much as I want you to be my wife."

She opened her mouth to protest, but Hank touched her lips to silence her. This was where the real test of his patience was going to come.

"Not now," he said. "We don't have to decide anything now." He grinned at her. "For one thing, I'm starving. For another, I think we need to get out of here, clear our heads a bit."

"You're not going back tonight?"

Her mixed feelings were totally transparent. "Not tonight," he said. "Disappointed?"

"Of course not, it's just that..." Her voice trailed off guiltily.

"It's just that you're scared you're vulnerable and that I'll talk you into something you don't really want to do," he said.

She frowned. "You're doing it again."

"Doing what?"

"Reading my mind."

He winked at her. "Just think how good I'll be at it when we're eighty."

Chapter Twelve

They were going to be together when they were eighty? Lizzy couldn't think that far ahead. She could barely envision what her life would be like in a few weeks when news of her pregnancy could no longer be concealed. If she thought Hank capable of bullying her into making a decision she would later regret, it was nothing compared to what the combined force of her father and brothers would do. She shuddered at the prospect of withstanding all that testosterone-driven pressure.

"Cold?" Hank asked at once.

She shot him an amused look. "Are you going to be this solicitous when I start pleading for pickles at 3:00 a.m.?"

"Of course," he promised. He studied her carefully. "Am I going to be there when these cravings kick in?"

Lizzy realized belatedly the trap she'd just set for herself. "I don't know," she said honestly. "Isn't that what we need to talk about?"

Hank nodded. "But first food. Where should we go?"

"How about Cuban? We're not that far from Little Havana. I think you'll like the food."

"If that's what you want, it's fine with me."

"Great," she said brightly. "I'll shower and we'll go."

Forty-five minutes later, they were seated in a restaurant that was noisy and jam-packed with a blend of Spanish-speaking families, Anglos and tourists. Versailles on Southwest Eighth Street—Calle Ocho—was one of her favorite places. The decor was bright and featured a lot of etched mirrors on the walls.

Lizzy explained the dishes on the menu, but Hank couldn't seem to focus. She knew exactly what his mind was on. His gaze kept straying to the babies at nearby tables. The expression on his face was a touching blend of awe and fascination.

"Why don't I order?" she said finally.

"Fine."

After the Cuban waitress had taken their order, Lizzy met Hank's gaze. "Okay, what's going on in that head of yours? You're watching those babies as if you've never seen one before."

"Knowing you're going to be a father changes

things. I was looking at those babies and wondering if their dads are as terrified of doing the wrong things as I am."

"Hank, you're going to be a wonderful father. You are kind and patient and strong. No man could set a better example for a child."

His jaw set in a way that was all too familiar. "And I will be there to set the example," he said quietly.

"Of course you will."

"I won't settle for being a part-time dad, Lizzy. If things between you and me were different, if we weren't suited at all, then maybe our child would be better off if we weren't together, but that's not the case here, is it?"

"No," she admitted slowly. "We get along great. What's your point?"

"Then there is no reason on earth for us not to get married and give this child the two-parent home he or she deserves," he said, looking directly into her eyes. "Is there?"

Lizzy flinched under that unwavering look. "Hank, it's not that simple."

"Okay, then, let's reduce it to the basics. You love me. I love you. We're having a baby. I want more than anything in this world for that baby to be born with my name, for us to make a home for him or her."

Lizzy regarded him with mounting frustration. "But what about me? What about my dreams?"

"We'll work it out."

"Until you can tell me how, I'm not going to marry you just because it's the easy thing to do."

"What about it being the right thing to do?" he asked quietly. "For one thing, try to imagine what my life expectancy is going to be once Cody and Luke and Jordan find out about the baby."

"Is that what this is all about?" She forced a grin. "No need to panic. I'll protect you."

Hank clearly was not amused. "How? With reason? Your brothers are not reasonable men. They act first and think later. I can't say that I'd blame them in this instance. If you were my sister, I'd kill the man who got you into this fix."

"Nobody is going to get killed, and you did not get me into this 'fix,' as you call it. I had a choice in the matter. What happened between us when I was home was my doing as much as yours."

"But I'm supposed to be the responsible, sensible one," he pointed out.

Lizzy's hackles rose. "And what am I?" she argued indignantly. "The airhead?"

"No, of course not."

"Drop it, Hank. You're just digging a very deep hole for yourself here."

"I'm just saying that I should have answers, but the only one I come up with you seem to be rejecting out of hand."

"Which is?"

"Get married."

"No," she said again.

"Dammit, Lizzy, I love you. You say you love

me. We're going to have a baby. We damned well ought to be married," he said with evident frustration.

Lizzy flinched at the mounting anger in his voice. "Be reasonable," she pleaded.

"Me? It seems to me that I am the only one around here who is being reasonable."

That did it. Lizzy stood up. "I knew it," she said, scowling at him. "I knew you were going to try to bully me into marrying you. Well, I'm not going to do it, so you can just get that idea out of your head once and for all."

With that, she turned and marched out of the restaurant, back straight, head held high. She was very much aware of the curious gazes following her and of Hank's muttered oath as he tossed some money on the table and sprinted after her.

"Lizzy," he shouted over the din of voices.

Lizzy was frantically trying to jam the key into her car's lock when Hank caught up with her.

"Lizzy," he said more quietly. "I'm sorry."

"No, you're not. You're like every male in my family. When you don't get your way right off, you turn stubborn and mule headed and sneaky. I wouldn't be a bit surprised if you didn't deliberately sabotage one of those condoms we used."

The silence that fell was so thick she wondered for a moment if she'd gone too far. Finally, she dared a glance into Hank's face. He was staring at her with astonishment and maybe just the tiniest trace of hurt in his eyes.

"If you think for a single minute that I would do something so underhanded," he began quietly, "then we are in serious trouble."

He regarded her steadily until she finally blushed and looked away.

"I'm sorry," she said eventually. "I know this was just one of those zillion-to-one accidents. Neither of us planned it."

"I hope you mean that."

She nodded. "It's just that I panic, and when I panic, I start lashing out. You're an easy target right now."

Hank jammed his hands into the pockets of his jeans as if to keep himself from reaching for her. "You know, darlin', you're not the only one who's been blindsided here. I found out about this today. You've had days to get used to the idea of having a baby, to think about what's best. I'm scrambling for the right answers and I keep locking on the most obvious one. If there's a better alternative, try it on me."

She regarded him miserably. "I don't have one," she confessed unhappily. "Maybe we don't have to have all the answers tonight."

"Maybe not," he agreed.

He opened his arms then, and Lizzy stepped into them and rested her head on his shoulder, breathing in the familiar, reassuring, male scent of him. With all the millions of things she didn't know right now, this was not one of them. This was real and right. Loving Hank was right.

"Do you want to go back in and finish your dinner?" he asked eventually. "I told the waitress not to take anything away, that we might be back."

Even if she weren't very conscious of the baby's need for nourishment, her growling stomach would have answered for her. "Sure," she said, then regarded Hank hopefully. "Do you think they'll bring me extra pickles for the *media noche* sandwich?"

Hank grinned. "If they won't, I'll buy the whole blasted jar."

"Don't go that far," she said. "I'm still not sure I like pickles. I never did before. All of a sudden, though, I just seem to have this craving for them."

"How many more months is this going to go on?" Hank wondered aloud.

Lizzy chuckled at his bewildered expression. "Nine is pretty much standard," she reminded him. "Don't despair, though. You've already missed the first few weeks."

Hank's expression sobered. "I know you meant that as a consolation, darlin', but it's not. It just reinforces my determination not to miss a single second of the next eight months or so."

She heard the grim determination in his voice and realized that she might be able to delay Hank from forcing her into a rash decision, but it would only be postponing the inevitable. He wasn't going to give up on marriage. Not in a million years.

And the pitiful truth was, she wasn't at all certain she wanted him to. That scared her most of all.

* * *

It was early evening by the time they got back to Lizzy's apartment and not quite dark. Rather than heading inside, Hank took her hand, tucked it through the crook of his arm and began to stroll toward the main hospital. An idea had struck him earlier in the afternoon, and now seemed like the perfect time to act on it. He sensed that Lizzy's resolve was weakening and he intended to use whatever weapons were at his disposal to assure that she came to see things his way. The ring he'd bought right before leaving Texas had been burning a hole in his pocket. He wanted to give it to her now more than ever.

"Where are we going?" Lizzy asked, but without really balking.

"Just for a stroll," he told her innocently.

"This isn't a neighborhood for strolling," she warned him.

"And we're not going that far."

He led her to the hospital's main entrance, then stepped inside the lobby, which was still bustling with visitors and staff.

"Wait right here," he told Lizzy as he went to talk to a clerk at the information desk.

When he came back, Lizzy regarded him warily. "What on earth are we doing here?"

"Just come with me, okay?"

"Why?"

"Humor me."

Lizzy could have balked then, but not without creating a scene. Hank saw the stirring of her curiosity. In fact, he was counting on it.

"Okay," she said eventually, and followed him to a bank of elevators.

He punched the button for the floor the clerk had indicated and spotted the first glimmer of understanding in Lizzy's eyes. When the doors opened, they were on the huge obstetrical floor, just down the hall from the nursery. Hank turned and led her to the window through which parents could watch their newborns.

A grin spread slowly across her face as she stared at the rows of babies, some of them squalling mightily, others right beside them sound asleep. He watched as her hands slid instinctively to her own belly, then reached over and covered them with his own.

He waited until she looked up at him, before saying quietly, "One of these days we're going to have a little guy or a little girl just like these. It's not a fantasy, Lizzy. It's not going to go away. The baby growing inside you is going to be front and center in our lives. We have to make the best possible decision before that happens. We have to know where we stand with each other and how we're going to cope with this incredible miracle God has given us. We can't keep putting it off and hope time will take care of it, which is why I think we should get married."

He took the jewelry box from his pocket but before he could remove the diamond, she placed her hand over his.

"I understand why you're doing this," she whispered, tears shining in her eyes. "But the decision has to be one we both can live with, Hank. It's not as simple as getting a marriage license and saying the vows. That's over in the blink of an eye. We have to live with everything that comes after.''

"It can be as simple or as complicated as we make it,'' he argued.

"Okay, let me ask you this. Right before I left Texas, you decided not to ask me to marry you because you knew in the end, I would only resent you for making me choose, right?''

"Yes,'' he conceded, not liking the tack she had taken at all because he could see where it was heading, and it sure as heck wasn't toward the altar. "What's your point?''

"Nothing's changed. Backing me into a corner is no way to start a marriage. The resentment will be a given, just as you predicted it would be.''

"There's a baby to consider now. That changes everything.'' He decided the time had come to hammer home his point. "How will you manage if you don't marry me? Have you considered that? Will you carry the baby to class with you?'' he pressed. "What about when you're on duty at the hospital? Will you haul the baby along? Or are you counting on Kelsey being a live-in baby-sitter? She might have other ideas.''

Lizzy looked shaken by the questions. "I don't have all the answers. All I can see is that you're asking me to make a huge sacrifice, to give up medicine, come home and be a wife and mother.''

Hank's temper flared, despite his intentions to stay

calm. "Would being my wife and the mother of our child be such a god-awful thing?"

"No, of course not."

"Then you're just being selfish," he accused. "You're being Harlan Adams's baby girl again, believing that you're entitled to everything you want and what's right for everybody else doesn't mean a damned thing. If you think you're turning this baby of mine over to some nanny to raise, you're crazy. I'll fight you for custody first."

Lizzy visibly reeled under the bitter accusation and the threat. "You won't take this baby away from me, Hank. You can forget that right now. And if you feel that way about me, if I'm such a terrible person and you hold me in such low esteem, why would you want to marry me in the first place?"

"Because I love you, dammit." Frustration had him shouting.

"Well, I love you, too," she shouted back.

A nurse stepped into the hallway and pressed a finger to her lips. "Shh. This is a hospital. Not a Vegas wedding chapel."

Hank offered a rueful apology, then turned back to Lizzy.

"We're not going to settle this tonight, are we?" he concluded, awash with regrets for letting the fight escalate and for not having options they could both live with.

"I guess not."

"Then let's go sleep on it. Maybe one of us will

come up with a brainstorm before morning. If not tomorrow morning, then the next day.''

"Or the next," Lizzy said, sounding fatalistic.

Hank tucked a finger under her chin. "We will work this out, darlin'. I promise you that."

Lizzy didn't look convinced, but she did take his hand when he offered it, and that night, when they crawled into her narrow bed, she trustingly fitted herself to his body and went off to sleep with his arms around her.

Hank was awake for hours, though, trying to untangle the complicated mess they'd made of their lives. He'd meant what he'd said about fighting her for custody before he'd let a stranger raise his child, but that was only a last resort. Surely there were better solutions.

Reduced to its simplest, black-and-white terms, there was only one answer: marriage. But getting Lizzy down the aisle was going to take more ingenuity than he possessed alone.

It was going to require the expertise of a master manipulator like her daddy.

For the next forty-eight hours, Lizzy did little except eat, go to her classes and talk to Hank. They hashed over their options a thousand times. And by the time he had to leave for Texas, they were no closer to a solution they could live with than they had been when he'd first shown up.

Kelsey had been a saint. She had refereed arguments when asked, but mostly she had stayed away and given them the space they needed to wrestle with the dilemma in which they'd found themselves.

"I'll be home in a month," Lizzy said as Hank distractedly mashed his cornflakes into a sodden mess. "We'll have the whole summer to work this out."

He pushed aside the cereal and lifted his gaze to hers. "In the meantime, is this our secret? Or do you intend to tell your folks?"

Lizzy shook her head at once. "I can't tell Daddy about this now. I don't know how he'll react."

"Oh, I think you do," Hank said dryly. "Harlan can't wait for you to give him another grandbaby. He'll be over the moon about the news."

"Yes, and he'll be on your side about the two of us getting married right away."

"More than likely," Hank agreed, looking as if he considered that an atomic-caliber secret weapon.

"Which is why he is not to know until you and I have reached a decision." She leveled a look straight at him. "Are we clear on that?"

"I will not discuss this with your father," he promised.

She regarded him suspiciously. "Or anyone else in my family."

He grinned. "Okay, darlin'. I will not discuss it with a single living soul. Does that cover enough ground?"

"I suppose." She glanced at the clock. "It's time. Please let me drive you to the airport."

"No. You have a class and I can take a taxi."

Suddenly, she didn't want him to go. Having him here, even though they'd spent most of the time arguing about the future, had been wonderfully reassuring. No matter how things turned out, no matter what decision they eventually reached, they were in this together. And, as she'd known for years, if ever she was in trouble, Hank Robbins was the kind of rock-steady man she'd want in her corner.

"At least let me go downstairs with you, then," she said. "I'll get my books so I can go on to class."

A few minutes later, they stood outside waiting for the taxi. It was a gorgeous spring day with the sky a brilliant blue and the air already thick with the first hint of summer's humidity.

Hank reached over and trailed his thumb along her jaw. "I'm glad I came and I'm glad you told me the truth about the baby."

"I would have told you even if you hadn't come," Lizzy said. "I was just trying to figure things out first."

"We will figure them out, darlin'." He grinned ruefully. "Maybe not on my preferred timetable, but we will figure them out. You can count on that."

A lump formed in her throat. "I can count on you, can't I?"

"Always."

Before she could say more, the cab pulled to the curb. After that, everything was rushed—Hank's kiss, the cab's departure, the wave of loneliness that washed over her.

She realized then how Hank must have felt the

times she had walked away. There was one huge difference, though. He had always let her go willingly and with his blessing. For all intents and purposes, she had sent him packing. She only prayed that when she got back to Texas in a few weeks, he would still be there waiting for her with open arms and not a court order demanding custody of their child the minute she gave birth.

Chapter Thirteen

The next few weeks were among the longest of Hank's life. He was counting the minutes until Lizzy came home for the summer. His mind kept wandering, imagining her with the legendary inner glow of a mother-to-be. Would her pregnancy be showing by then? Would they have any time at all to work out a plan on their own before the entire Adams clan thrust themselves into the midst of the dilemma and made plans for them?

"Hey, boss? Everything okay?"

Hank's head snapped up at Pete's words. He'd forgotten entirely that the other man was waiting for his decision about whether they needed to hire a private investigator to get to the bottom of the troubling incidents that had been taking place around the ranch.

There had been a few more since his return from Miami, mostly minor annoyances, but definitely worrisome in total.

"I'm sorry, Pete. My mind wandered."

"Seems to be doing that a lot lately," the older man noted. "Wouldn't have anything to do with that pretty little doc, would it? When is she coming home?"

Hank grinned. Pete and the men had taken to calling Lizzy "doc" ever since she'd saved Billy-Clyde after that bull had gored him. "A couple of days, I suppose," he said with feigned nonchalance, even though he knew to the precise minute when her flight was due in.

"Don't have it quite calculated down to the second yet?" Pete taunted.

Hank bristled at the accuracy of the man's guesswork. "You know, Pete, you may be a hell of a foreman, but I could do better," he threatened with mock sincerity.

"Not in this lifetime," the old man countered, clearly undaunted. "And not for what you're willing to pay."

"Let's face it, you just stick around for Mrs. Wyndham's cooking."

Pete grinned. "She does make a mighty fine biscuit. If she weren't already a married lady, I do believe I'd court her for those biscuits and her blueberry pie." His gaze narrowed. "Now, back to that private eye. I'm thinking we should bring him in here and put a rest to these little incidents before they get out of hand.''

Hank thought of Lizzy and the possible danger to her if he failed to take the mischief seriously enough.

"Do it," he said, vowing to warn her that she was not to go traveling around his property or even her own family's unaccompanied until this was resolved. There was no way in hell he was taking chances on her safety or the baby's.

"Are you going to tell Cody what you're up to?" Pete asked. "He might want to be in on it, too. A couple of things have happened over at White Pines, as well. There's a snake of the human variety sneaking around here, all right. I'd bet my life on it.''

"I'll talk to Cody," Hank promised. "I'll ride over there as soon as we're done here. How's Billy-Clyde doing?''

"He should be back to work in a week or so. He's been worried you wouldn't want him back since he won't be up to full speed for a while yet, but I told him we always take care of our own around here and he became one of ours the day you hired him.''

"Exactly right," Hank said.

"Could you maybe stop by the bunkhouse and tell him that? It might reassure him.''

"I'll do it on my way out," Hank promised. "Okay, then, if that's it, I'll head on over to see Cody.''

"I'll fill you in on what happens with the private eye as soon as he agrees to be on the payroll.''

Hank gave him a terse nod. It wouldn't be soon enough to suit him.

After a brief visit with Billy-Clyde, he saddled up and rode toward the neighboring ranch, hoping to find Cody in the office, instead of off someplace. But instead of running into Cody in the office at the back of the main house, he found Harlan behind the desk, booted feet resting atop the cluttered mahogany surface, a phone tucked against his ear.

He looked hale and robust for a man of his years and very much back in command. Obviously, his recovery was just about complete. Hank rapped on the door, then waited until Harlan acknowledged him with a beckoning wave.

"Hey, boy, what brings you by?" he said when he got off the phone.

"Looking for Cody, actually, but it's a pleasure to find you up and back in the middle of things."

Harlan grinned. "Doubt Cody would agree with you. He says I'm in here messing up his filing system."

Hank studied the haphazard arrangement of papers, a good number of which had tumbled, helter-skelter onto the floor. "System?" he asked doubtfully.

"My point exactly. The place is a gosh-darned mess. He says all the important stuff is in that danged computer of his anyway. Besides, he claims he's got more-important fish to fry these days." He gave Hank a canny look. "Any idea what he could mean by that?"

Hank's spirits sank. Unfortunately, he suspected he knew exactly what was on Cody's mind and it answered the very question he'd come to ask.

"You do know something, don't you?" Harlan said, immediately picking up on Hank's reaction. "What is it?"

"I can't be sure."

"Then try the guesswork out on me. I'm looking for something I can wrestle with to keep my mind active. The newspapers just get me riled up."

"I'm not sure I should."

Harlan glowered. "Don't you start treating me like an invalid, too. I've had about all I can take of people tiptoeing around me like the least little thing will send me into a relapse. If there's something going on around here, I need to know about it. Until they put me in the ground, White Pines is still my ranch."

Hank understood his frustration. He also understood that even though Harlan had turned the day-to-day operations over to Cody, it was his heart and soul that had taken the run-down family home and turned it into a thriving cattle operation. Harlan Adams had given Hank an example to live by when he'd bought the dilapidated operation up the road.

"Okay, I can only tell you about what's been happening at my place." He elaborated on several incidents.

Harlan's gaze narrowed. "And you think the same sort of thing's been going on around here?"

"I wouldn't be surprised. In fact, that's why I came by this morning. I wanted to talk to Cody about it. See if he wanted to go in with me on hiring an investigator to check things out.''

"When exactly did these incidents start?"

"A couple of months back."

Harlan's expression turned pensive. "Around the time you and Lizzy started getting serious," he said thoughtfully.

Hank started at the connection the old man was drawing. "What the hell are you saying?"

"Just that the timing is downright fascinating, don't you think?"

"There's no connection," Hank insisted. "There can't be. The timing's pure coincidence."

"We'll see," Harlan said enigmatically. "You get that private investigator on the job and then send him over to have a chat with me. I don't want to start tossing around accusations without any evidence, but I damned well want him to start looking in the right direction."

Harlan didn't have to say any more. To his deep regret, Hank was suddenly able to follow his unspoken logic. He knew exactly who was implicated— that sleazy oilman who'd been trying his damnedest to seduce Lizzy at that party.

But why? Why would Brian Lane resort to making mischief? Most of the incidents could be dismissed as no more than childish revenge, he supposed, but there had to be more. He met Harlan's gaze directly.

"What do you know about Brian that I don't?" he demanded.

"Enough to know that he's a fool, and a fool with money and a sick soul is dangerous."

"Is this about Lizzy, then?"

"Maybe," Harlan conceded, then surprised Hank by adding, "Maybe not."

"What are you thinking?"

"It could be about the land," Harlan said. "My hunch is that he saw her as a means to get the land around here. You've gotten in his way."

Hank was about to ask about why an oilman would want ranch land, but the answer hit him squarely between the eyes. "Oil," he said softly.

Harlan nodded.

"But if there's oil here, doesn't he know that Jordan would never let it fall into a competitor's hands?"

"He knows that this land is off limits for anyone exploring for oil, even my own son. I haven't spent my whole life building this into a proud cattle empire only to see it pockmarked with a bunch of oil rigs. But if my land is rich with crude, then yours probably is, too. If Brian can drive you off and get Lizzy to marry him, he'll have his foot in the door at both places and he's the kind who'll kick it clean down to get what he wants."

"If he tries getting his blasted toe through the door, I'll cut the damned thing off for him," Hank said fiercely. "That land is mine and so is Lizzy."

He stopped pacing and noted that Harlan was grinning.

"About time you made yourself clear on that

point," the old man said. "I was beginning to wonder if I'd pegged you wrong."

Hank shot him a rueful look. "I'm not the problem, sir. It's your daughter. Unfortunately, she has a mind of her own and a timetable that would drive a teetotaler to drink."

"Then I guess you'd best get busy persuading her that timetables don't mean a danged thing, unless they're for trains or airlines. Human beings ought to be flexible."

"With all due respect, sir, she's an Adams. If the woman's stubborn, she got it from you."

Harlan began to chuckle. "Yes, I suppose she did. Well, you've never struck me as the sort of man to give up just because there's a little roadblock in his path. Or am I wrong?"

"No, sir, you are not wrong," Hank said with grim determination. "Call the caterers, because there's going to be a wedding right here at White Pines before the summer's out, and that's a promise."

Lizzy dreaded going home. She hated the thought of facing her family. Not that they would judge her. She knew better than that. But they would have a thing or two to say about what ought to happen next. She was relieved when Hank said he would drive over and meet her flight in Dallas. Not that he didn't have his own opinions about the future, but she'd already dealt with him. So far she'd managed to stand up to him just fine.

Of course, he was getting impatient. She'd heard it in his voice the past few times they'd talked. If she didn't give in to his way of thinking soon, he'd be as formidable to deal with as Luke, Jordan, Cody and her father combined.

She spotted him the second she walked off the plane. He was lounging against a railing in the gate area, his booted feet crossed at the ankles, his jeans a snug fit over those long legs and narrow hips, a Stetson pulled low over his brow. There were other men similarly dressed in the waiting area, but nobody on earth personified the cowboy mystique the way this man did. Lizzy could see it in the way every woman who walked past gave him a second look. She wanted to throttle every one of them.

"Okay, cowboy, you can stop posing now," she said. "And don't tell me you weren't aware of the impression you were making."

He regarded her with innocent blue eyes. "Impression?"

"On the ladies. You had them ogling."

"You sound just a smidge jealous, darlin'."

"Do not."

"Do, too," he said, and swept her into a hug and spun her around. He delivered a long, breath-stealing kiss that wiped away every single trace of envy in her body. He stood back and regarded her, his expression smug. "Feel better now?"

"You can't get out of this with a piddly old kiss," she retorted.

"You call that kiss piddly?" he said with pure masculine indignation.

She studied him thoughtfully. "Can you do better?"

He grinned then. "Not in public. Any better and I'd get us arrested."

"Big talk, cowboy."

His expression sobered. "Ah, darlin', it is good to have you home again." He held her at arm's length.

"Hank, what on earth are you doing?"

"Surveying."

"I'm not a piece of land you're thinking of buying," she protested.

"No, you're the mother of my baby. I want to see if it shows." He turned her sideways. "Damn."

"What?"

"You're still downright skinny. Haven't you been eating properly? You can't starve yourself to death. The baby needs sustenance." He held his hand a few inches from her waist. "I expected you to be out to here by now."

Lizzy rolled her eyes. "If this is the way you're going to be for the next few months, I'm getting on a plane back to Miami right this second."

Hank glowered. "Over my dead body."

"Well, then, stop fussing." But even as she uttered the warning, some small part of her blossomed at the concern in his voice and at the possessive way his gaze slid over her. She had always been loved, always been surrounded by people who cared heart and soul for her well-being, but this was different.

This was what it felt like to be cherished. How could she turn her back on this?

"Hank?"

"Yes."

"Does anyone at home suspect?"

"Not as far as I know."

"How are we going to tell them?"

"That's up to you. More to the point, what are we going to tell them?" He turned to study her intently. "Are we going to tell them about the baby? Or are we just going to tell them that we can't wait any longer and we're getting married?"

Lizzy sighed. "I've been over this and over it. I'm still no closer to knowing what's right than I was when you left Miami."

Hank's expression turned resigned. "Then I guess we take it one day at a time for now."

"I'm sorry," Lizzy said. "I know that's not what you wanted to hear."

"No," he agreed. "And in a few more weeks, it won't be good enough, not for me and not for anyone in your family. They're going to want answers, Lizzy. We all are."

"Don't you think I want answers, too?" she retorted heatedly. "This isn't exactly a picnic for me, either. I'm just trying to do what's right, Hank, not just for the baby, but for all of us. And I think you can forget having much time before we have to fill my parents in. They're going to figure out something's up by suppertime. They always do."

He slammed the palm of his hand against the steering wheel. "I'll tell you what's right, dammit. The parents of this baby ought to be married. That's what's right."

"Not if we'll be divorced within a year," she flung right back.

There was a hard, unyielding look in Hank's eyes when he met her gaze. "You've got that right. Because once you and I are married, darlin', it's going to be for keeps."

Lizzy trembled under the fire in his eyes. That kind of commitment was something she'd dreamed of all her life. It was the kind of commitment that bound her parents together, the kind she wanted as an example for her own children. And it was what she wanted with Hank, a happily-ever-after, till-death-do-us-part commitment. Just not yet, her head screamed. She needed a few more years to finish her medical training.

But fate wasn't giving her a choice in the matter, it seemed. There was a baby on the way now, and he or she sure as hell wasn't going to wait around for her to finish med school, an internship and a residency before putting in an appearance, not unless she pulled off a pregnancy for the record books.

It would be so easy to say yes to Hank, to simply give in and claim his love and his support, but then what? How long would it be before the resentment kicked in and the little fights over nothing began to eat away at their love?

Hank glanced over. "Lizzy? Are you feeling okay?"

Unless heartsick counted, she was fine. "I'm okay," she said wearily.

"I don't want you worrying about telling your family by yourself," he said. "Whether it's today or a couple of weeks from now, I'll be right there beside you. I want them to know I'm accepting my responsibility."

She grinned halfheartedly at that. "Hank, there would never be a doubt in their minds about that. I'm the one they're going to want to shake some sense into."

"I won't let them do that, either," he promised. "Look, honey, I know this isn't easy. If it were, I'd have dragged you in front of a preacher by now. But there is a solution. We just have to find it."

"Unless you've got one up your sleeve, we're out of luck," she said. "We're only a few miles from White Pines, and one look at my face and Mother and Daddy are going to know something's wrong."

He regarded her with obvious astonishment. "Then you intend to tell them straight out?"

She shrugged. "I might as well. It won't take them long to guess, anyway."

Hank nodded. "Then I'll be right there, too."

"I'm not so sure that's a good idea."

"Well, I am and that's final."

"Okay, if you insist, but I hope you've got your running shoes on, because you might have to make a quick getaway."

"Darlin', one thing you should know about me by now, I never, ever run from a little trouble."

"How about from a whole passel of loaded shotguns?"

Hank paled a bit at that, but his jaw squared and his expression remained resolute. "Not even then."

Oddly enough, now that he'd said it, Lizzy knew that was exactly what she'd been counting on all along. With Hank by her side, she could face anything, even her parents' disappointment and displeasure.

What she wasn't prepared for was finding the whole household in total chaos.

Chapter Fourteen

"There's a fire at Hank's place," Lizzy's mother shouted, waving them down as Lizzy and Hank drove up in front of White Pines. "Hank, you'd better get over there right away."

Hank stared at her as if he couldn't quite comprehend what she was saying. Lizzy jumped in to fill the heavy, shocked silence.

"What happened?" she asked. "Does anyone know yet?"

"Pete says it started in the barn and flared up quick. As dry as the weather's been, they're afraid it could spread to the house," her father explained, his expression filled with sympathy. "Cody and Jordan are on the way, along with Justin and Harlan Patrick and all the men we can spare. Luke's sending who-

ever he can from his ranch. I've got a helicopter going over to pick them up.''

He reached out and squeezed Hank's shoulder.
''I'm sorry, son. It doesn't look good, but everyone
will do what they can. If your place can be saved,
we'll do it, and if it can't be, then you can count on
all of us to help you rebuild it.''

''Oh, my God,'' Lizzy murmured watching the
look of desperation spread over Hank's face. She
knew what the ranch meant to him and she wasn't
about to let him face this alone. ''I'm coming with
you.''

That got his attention. ''No way,'' Hank said, his
jaw set stubbornly. ''Get out of the truck, Lizzy.
You're staying here.''

She stayed right where she was. ''No, if someone's injured, I can help.''

''She has a point,'' her mother said quietly. ''I'll
come, too.''

Hank sent Lizzy a pleading look. ''But the
baby...'' he whispered. ''If anything happens to the
baby, I'll never forgive myself.''

Oblivious to the shocked looks being exchanged
by her parents, Lizzy covered Hank's white-knuckled
grip on the steering wheel with her hand. ''It will be
okay. I promise we won't get in any danger. Now,
stop wasting time and let's go.''

''I'm coming, too,'' her father declared, already
moving off toward his pickup.

''Absolutely not,'' Lizzy and her mother protested
in unison.

"I'll stay back with Lizzy," he said, his gaze on his wife steady. "In case she needs me."

"But—" Hank began.

"Just go, dammit. This fire's not going to sit still while we hang around here arguing," her father said, already climbing into his own truck with Janet right on his heels.

Hank threw his truck into gear and took off toward home. In the distance, gray smoke was billowing over the horizon. "I swear to God if that low-down son of a bitch had anything to do with this, he will pay."

As the implication of his words registered, Lizzy stared at him in shock. "You think this fire was deliberately set?"

"I'd bet on it," he said, his expression grim. "Too many things have happened lately for this to be a coincidence."

"But who would do such a thing?" she demanded. Her gaze narrowed as she studied his grim expression. "You think you know that, too, don't you?"

His silence was confirmation enough. His admission that this wasn't the first suspicious incident made her uneasy. Could this be tied in with Hank's accident a few weeks earlier? And how many more little accidents had happened that she knew nothing about?

"Who, Hank? Who's in back of this?"

"Let's just say it's someone who doesn't know when to quit."

By then, it was too late to try to pry answers out

of him. He pulled his truck to a stop upwind of the fire in an area that looked for the moment, anyway, to be safe enough. Though smoke was still billowing, it appeared that so far the worst of the blaze had been contained to the barn.

"Lizzy, promise me you won't come any closer," Hank insisted. "And at the first sign that the wind is shifting, you will take the truck and go back to White Pines."

She could see how torn he was about leaving her at all. "Go," she said. "I'll be fine. I'll just get first-aid supplies from the house and come right back here. If anyone's injured, direct them this way."

Hank froze. "You are not to go near the house, dammit. It looks safe enough now, but fire's unpredictable. One little spark and it could flare up all over again. The house could go next."

"No," she said quietly. "You'll have the fire under control long before it gets that far. Look, Hank. Look at the barn. There are very few flames left. It's mostly smoldering now."

"And you and I both know how quickly that could change with the wind whipping around and everything dry as tinder. Stay here, dammit. I'll get whatever supplies you need and send them out here."

She could see there was no arguing with him, so she stayed where she was, relaxing only after he'd gone. Seated on the tailgate of the pickup, her gaze following Hank, she was only dimly aware of her father and mother coming to sit on either side of her.

"It's going to be okay, darlin' girl," her father

promised. "It's just a barn. We'll all pitch in and have it rebuilt for him in no time."

"What if I'm wrong, though? What if it does spread and take the house?"

"Then we'll rebuild that, too," he said. "You know how folks around here stick together in a crisis, and Hank's practically family now. We'll do what's right by him."

"You won't be able to rebuild Hank's spirit so easily," she said. "This ranch means the world to him. He's a lot like Luke, Daddy. He could have stayed at home and taken over his father's operation, but he needed to prove he could succeed on his own. You remember what this place was like before he fixed it up. It was a wreck. He's turned it into a home."

"As long as you are safe and his cattle are safe, Hank will have what it takes to start over," her mother said, then gave her a pointed look. "And this baby you're carrying will give him a reason to look forward."

Lizzy was startled that her mother had guessed, then recalled Hank's outburst back at White Pines. She searched her mother's face for signs of anger. "You're not furious with me?"

"You're my daughter. I'll always love you, no matter what. This won't be the first baby that got a jump on its parents' marriage."

Lizzy turned to her father, fearful of the condemnation she might read in his eyes. "And you?"

"Do you even need to ask? All I want is your

happiness. Just tell me when the wedding is and I'll be the proudest man in the church.''

Tears leaked from her eyes and spilled down her cheeks. ''You two are the most incredible parents a woman could ever have.'' She decided now was not the time to tell them that there was no wedding date just yet or that she was the one holding out. There would be time enough to get into all that when the fire was out and things had settled down again.

Lizzy peered through the increasingly heavy smoke trying to catch sight of Hank, but all she saw were shadows rushing about with hoses and buckets, dousing the new flare-ups, and men with shovels digging a break line to keep the fire from ever reaching the nearby ranch house.

Mrs. Wyndham emerged from the chaos bearing first-aid supplies. ''Hank says you may be needing these and that I'm to stay and help.''

She was as calm and unflappable as ever. Lizzy had the feeling that it would take a lot more than a fire to rattle Hank's housekeeper.

''Do you have any idea what happened?'' Lizzy asked her.

The housekeeper shook her head. ''I never saw a thing. Pete was in with me having his supper when we heard a shout from one of the men. Next thing I knew, all hell had broken loose. They had me call over to your place and told me to get what I could out of the house just in case the fire started spreading that way. I've loaded Pete's pickup with all the valuables I could carry and moved it down the lane.''

Her gaze sought out Hank in the distance, and she shook her head. "That poor boy. Every rancher has a hard life, but Hank's worked harder than most to make a go of this place. He's always had something to prove to himself."

She glanced at Lizzy. "As if there was ever any doubt about him measuring up," she said fiercely. "There's not a man around who can hold a candle to him. I don't know what I would have done when C.J. took sick and had to retire, if it weren't for Hank giving me this job. He gave Pete a break when his last employer decided he was too old to work. Hank surely doesn't deserve a thing like this."

"Were they able to get all the livestock out of the barn?" Lizzy's father asked.

Mrs. Wyndham nodded. "Most of the horses were in the corral. The men just turned them loose. I suppose they'll wander back on their own sooner or later."

"I see," her father said, his expression thoughtful.

Lizzy recognized that tone. She could tell from her mother's expression that she did, too.

"Harlan, what are you thinking?" her mother asked. "I know that tone of voice."

"You ever heard of an accidental fire that gets started when it's least likely to harm an animal?"

"There's no accounting for when a short will set off a fire," her mother said.

"It just seems a little too coincidental to me. I'd say someone wanted to do some damage but didn't want to be blamed for taking any lives, not even the horses'.''

"Then you're saying this was deliberately set, too," Lizzy said, stunned by her father's confirmation of Hank's own theory, which she'd badly wanted to dismiss as absurd.

"I am and, more than likely, by that same weasel who's been behind all the other mischief around here."

"Who?"

"Brian Lane, of course."

Lizzy's mouth gaped. "What are you saying, Daddy? Surely you don't think Brian would burn down Hank's barn. It doesn't make any sense."

"But that's exactly what I think," he countered. "And if Hank finds out that's who it was, there won't be a place on this earth that man can hide."

"But why?" Lizzy asked, though the sinking sensation in the pit of her stomach told her she already knew some, if not all of it. "It's because of me, isn't it?"

Her father regarded her intently. "Don't you dare go blaming yourself for this. The man had an agenda, that's all. You were an intended victim, same as Hank. It had more to do with oil than love, I can guarantee you that."

"But if Hank loses everything, I'll still be partly to blame," she whispered, staring toward the devastation of the barn.

"You will not," her mother said, taking her firmly by the shoulders and forcing her to meet her gaze.

"No one's to blame but Brian." She shot a look at her husband. "*If* this was his doing in the first place. I still say your father is making something out of nothing and that he's going to get sued for slander for dragging the man's name through the mud the way he's been doing the last few hours."

Lizzy forced a smile at the defense of Brian. It was proof of her mother's generous nature. "You always did see the good in people. For an attorney who dealt with her fair share of guilty criminals, it's a pretty amazing trait."

"Yes, well, sometimes you have to look beyond the obvious."

"And sometimes, evil's just plain evil," her father contradicted. "I never liked that man. I told Jordan that, too, on more than one occasion. I suspect that's why Jordan never made him a part of his company, even though Brian hinted at it often enough."

"Daddy, if you felt that way about Brian, why in heaven's name did you even invite him to White Pines?"

He shot her a rueful look. "Because he's the kind of man men tend to take an instant dislike to. Heaven help me, I figured if anyone could get Hank to admit to himself how he felt about you, it would be Brian. Thank goodness that part worked, at least."

"Oh, Harlan, when will you stop meddling?" her mother whispered with a sigh. "Can't you see that's what set all of this in motion?"

"It also got Lizzy and Hank headed along the right

path,'' he argued, his expression intractable. ''And I won't apologize for that.''

They were still debating the point when Lizzy slipped away and headed out across Hank's property on the shortcut back to White Pines. The walk would do her good. She needed to think and she needed to be alone to do it. Her mother and Mrs. Wyndham could cope with whatever injuries turned up among the men fighting the blaze at Hank's, and the paramedics had been arriving from neighboring counties for some time now.

None of them had a treatment for what ailed her, though. She doubted there was a medical text available that had a treatment for guilt. No matter what her parents said, she'd set all of this in motion—she and her father—with their games to make Hank jealous.

It was time—way past time, in fact—to grow up and take responsibility for her own actions, to get over the notion that all of her whims would be granted as they had been since childhood. She owed Hank for having set all of this into motion. Now it was payback time. Sometimes there simply were no easy choices or quick fixes. And sometimes love meant sacrificing a dream to do what was right.

By midnight the fire was out and the fatigue had set in. Though the women from the neighboring ranches had brought soup and sandwiches and coffee all during the evening, no one had really had time to sit down and take a break to enjoy them. Now they sat in the beds of pickups and on the ground, waiting to be sure that not a single spark was left to set off a whole new blaze and using the time to catch their collective breath.

"I will never be able to thank you all enough," Hank said to Cody, Luke, Jordan and the other men nearby.

"No thanks necessary," Cody said. "You'd do the same if one of us was in trouble. That's just the way it is."

"My question is how are we going to prove who was behind this?" Jordan asked.

"The truth is we may never know," Luke said bluntly.

"We'll know," Hank said, unwilling to let it rest until they did. "I am going to look that sick son of a bitch straight in the eye and demand an honest answer. I'll know if Brian Lane is lying."

"And then what? Are you going to turn him over to the law?" Cody asked.

"It won't do any good without proof," Justin said as he came up to join them. "You'll need evidence that will stand up in court, not all the suppositions and slander I've heard being tossed around here the past few minutes."

Jordan frowned at his son. "Okay, Justin, you're so dead-set on being a lawman, you find the proof," he challenged. "Then maybe I'll take this notion of yours seriously."

Justin stilled and stared at his father. Hank could feel the tension shimmering in the air between them.

Apparently, the others could feel it, too, because Luke said quietly, "Jordan, Justin doesn't need to prove his worth to you. If he wants to be a cop, then he needs your blessing, not a test he has to pass before you'll give it to him. Remember the hoops Daddy made you and me jump through."

"And we were stronger men because of it," Jordan declared, his expression set stubbornly.

"Even so, we both vowed we wouldn't do the same to our own kids," Luke countered. "Not that I did so well taking my own advice where Angela was concerned. My expectations drove her off and kept her away from Jessie and me for years. Learn from my mistakes, too, Jordan."

Jordan sighed. "Okay, you're right," he conceded with obvious reluctance. He faced Justin. "Still and all, catching Brian in his lies ought to guarantee you a place with the sheriff's department right here in Los Piños."

"Tate's eager to retire and run off to Arizona so he can play golf seven days a week. He's already guaranteed me a place," Justin retorted with a grin. "But I'll see what I can come up with just the same." He glanced at Hank. "Will you leave it to me for now? I swear to you I won't let Brian Lane get away with this if he's guilty."

Hank didn't want to agree. He wanted to find the other man and beat the truth out of him, but he nodded anyway. "For now," he agreed. He glanced toward the place where he'd left Lizzy hours earlier. His truck was still there, but there was no sign of her. A faint shiver of alarm raced through him when he couldn't spot her. "Has anybody seen Lizzy?"

"Not me," Cody said.

"Haven't seen Janet or Daddy in a while, either," Luke noted. "Their truck's gone. They've probably gone back to White Pines to get some rest. Why don't you give her a call over there, Hank? I'll bet Lizzy is waiting up to hear that everything's okay."

Hank shook his head. If Lizzy had gone home, it was because she needed the sleep. Since he couldn't tell her brothers why rest was so critical for her now, he said simply, "If she's with Harlan and Janet, she's in good hands. I'll catch up with her first thing in the morning. I'm going to get some sleep myself now. You men ought to head on home and do the same."

Cody shook his head. "Send the others home, but I think I'll stick around a little longer, if you don't mind."

"I might as well hang out till morning, too," Luke agreed.

"Count me in," Jordan and Justin said together.

Hank eyed them suspiciously. "Why? You don't think Brian will try again, do you?"

"I wouldn't put anything past that scum," Cody said angrily. "I'd like to get my hands on him myself. We're all here. We might as well keep an eye on things. If he sets foot on the place, one of us will spot him."

Hank gave him a grateful look. "Then you all go on inside and catch whatever sleep you can. I'll have

Mrs. Wyndham make me a fresh pot of coffee and I'll take first watch.''

The others all agreed and headed for the ranch house, all except Cody, who remained right where he was.

Hank studied him intently. ''Something on your mind?''

''You and Lizzy.''

''What about us?''

''I haven't heard anything about a wedding date.''

''We've had a few other things going on around here since she got home this afternoon,'' Hank stated.

''Have you set a date or not?'' Cody persisted.

Hank gave him a resigned smile. ''Not exactly.''

''But you've asked her?''

''Till I'm blue in the face,'' he said with frustration, then shrugged. ''She'll come around in her own good time. I'm counting on it.''

Cody grinned. ''Could be she needs a little nudge. Want me to talk to her? Better yet, I could have Melissa, Sharon Lynn, Jenny and the other women gang up on her.''

''I doubt that would do much good. If there's one thing I've learned about an Adams, they do things in their own sweet time and not even an act of God is going to rush them.''

Cody nodded. ''If you know that about us, then I suppose you and Lizzy will get on right well.'' His gaze narrowed. ''Just one thing.''

''What's that?''

"Don't follow my example and wait too long. Try to get her to the altar before the baby's born."

Hank stared at him in shock. "Is there anything you people don't know practically before it happens?"

Cody laughed. "I'm not omniscient, if that's what you're thinking. I had a minute alone with Daddy earlier. He told me you'd let it slip and that Lizzy had confirmed it."

"Then I'm surprised you didn't toss me in among the dying embers of that blaze."

"And rob my niece or nephew of a daddy? Not a chance." He leveled a steady look at Hank. "But I will hog-tie you and drag you into the church myself if need be."

"Hey," Hank protested. "I'm not the one who needs persuading. You made me an offer not a minute ago. Talk to your sister."

Cody shuddered, clearly less interested in such a discussion with the stakes escalating by the minute. "Oh, no, I think I'll leave her to Daddy, after all. She's his little girl. If she's going to listen to anyone, it'll be him."

"That may have been true once," Hank said. "But something tells me Lizzy's marching to her own drummer these days, and the rest of us are just going to have to wait until he starts playing our tune."

Chapter Fifteen

It had been forty-eight hours since the fire, and Hank had been caught up in a whirlwind of decisions. He'd also been beseiged by nosy insurance investigators, to say nothing of trying to round up all the horses that had scattered at the first whiff of smoke. In all the confusion, there had been no sign of Lizzy and no time to go looking for her.

He had a feeling he knew exactly what Lizzy's disappearing act the night of the fire meant. He'd seen the guilt in her eyes when he'd mentioned that Brian Lane might be behind the fire.

He also guessed that she was hiding out at home, trying to distance herself from him and the decisions that had to be made.

By midday of the third day after the fire, things

were settling back into a more normal routine. He and Cody and the others agreed that the danger from another fire was slim. Brian—if he was the one responsible—was lying low. Maybe he even knew by now that Justin was looking for clues that would implicate him. It wouldn't stay a secret for long around Los Piños that he was under suspicion for setting the blaze.

"Boss, the men and I were talking," Pete told him when he found Hank staring at the rubble. "We'll get to work on putting up a new barn in our spare time. If you'll get the lumber in here, we'll get started tonight."

Hank was touched by the offer. "That's not necessary," he told the older man. "I can hire a crew to do the job. You all have enough work."

"Yes, it is necessary. You've stood by each of us when we've had our troubles. Just look what you've done by keeping Billy-Clyde on the payroll when he hasn't been able to pull his weight. As for me, I'd be rocking on some porch, bored to tears, if you hadn't given me this job. We figure we owe you."

Hank could see that the offer meant a lot to his foreman. He held out his hand. "Thank you. Tell the men I appreciate what you're doing. I'll have the supplies you'll need here by tomorrow at the latest."

"Boss, one other thing. The men wanted me to tell you how much they appreciated the doc sticking around the other night. She's going to be busy as can be if she sets up practice around here. She's got a real gentle, reassuring way about her."

Hank smiled. She did, indeed. "I'll tell her that."

As soon as Pete had gone, Hank went inside and called the lumber company. They promised he'd have his delivery by morning, along with all the men they could spare, as well.

Mrs. Wyndham appeared in the doorway, hands on hips, her expression grim. "If you don't mind my saying so, you could do with some cleaning up," she chided. "When was the last time you passed under a shower?"

Hank grinned. "Not as many days ago as you're probably thinking, but I imagine I could do with another one."

"Then get on upstairs and take one. I'll have lunch on the table when you get down. Cody said he'd be back around then, and I expect we'll be seeing Luke and the others, as well. This arson business hasn't set well with any of them."

At the mention of arson, Hank's blood began to boil. It had taken all of his willpower to leave matters in Justin's hands, but if he didn't have answers soon, Hank was going after Brian himself. Unless he was made to pay for this, there was no telling what would come next.

By the time he got downstairs, the Adams men were all seated at his dining-room table. They fell silent when Hank walked in. Hank's gaze shot to Justin.

"What have you found out?"

"The fool didn't even have sense enough to buy the gasoline he used in the next county. Carl said he filled up three gallon containers at his pumps the very morning of the fire. Paid with his credit card, too. Now, could be he had a lot of lawn mowers to fill up or it could be he's got an old tractor that doesn't take much gas to operate, but I'm betting that gas came right out here. The insurance-company arson investigator agrees it was gasoline that got things started.''

''Surely the man's not that dumb,'' Hank said. ''If he intended to set a fire, wouldn't he have paid cash at least?''

''You would think so,'' Jordan agreed. ''But the way I figure it, maybe he wanted you to know who was behind it.''

''Why?'' Cody demanded.

''Payback for Lizzy,'' Luke said quietly. ''You stole something he wanted right in plain sight, and now he's done the same to you.''

''What kind of sick logic is that?'' Hank demanded. Then another terrifying thought struck. ''What about Lizzy? Will he go after her, try to claim her?''

Lizzy's brothers exchanged a solemn look that told Hank everything he needed to know. ''I'm going to White Pines.''

''Hank,'' Cody called out. ''Don't worry. He'll have to go through all of us to get to her.''

Hank didn't wait to see if the others intended to follow or not. He saddled his horse and raced for White Pines. Janet met him at the front door. ''Hank, what is it? The fire hasn't started up again, has it?''

"No, it's Lizzy. Is she here? I have to see her."

"She's upstairs resting."

"Are you sure?"

She regarded him uneasily. "Of course I'm sure. Where else would she be?"

"I just need to see that for myself. Please."

She stood aside. "Just don't wake her, okay. She's been restless. I don't think she's gotten much sleep the past few days."

Hank barely heard her. He was already sprinting up the stairs. He'd known for years which room Lizzy had. She'd pointed out the window once, hinting that she would scale the tree outside to meet him for a secret rendezvous if he were willing. He'd never taken her up on it, but he'd never forgotten which room it was. Sometimes late at night, he'd sat outside in the dark at his place and imagined he could see the light beckoning from that window.

When he got to the room, he stood silently and forced himself to calm down. He opened the door quietly and eased inside. The drapes were drawn, but even so the sunshine crept through a gap, casting just enough light for him to see that she was safely tucked under the covers. A sigh eased out of him then.

He edged closer and gazed down at her, a lump in his throat. Whatever it took, whatever compromises were necessary, she was going to be his, he vowed. He would not lose her or his baby, not to Brian's sick revenge, not to her own doubts. If that meant making a few sacrifices while she finished her medical studies, then so be it.

Satisfied at last that she was perfectly secure, he slipped out of the room and joined Janet at the foot of the stairs. He shrugged sheepishly at her puzzled expression.

"I got it into my head that Brian could come after her," he said. "Cody and the others were afraid of the same thing."

Janet shook her head. "Which explains why there are pickups barreling up the driveway even as we speak. This has to stop, Hank. Somebody has to deal with Brian, and I know who that someone is going to be."

Hank stared at the grim set of her jaw. "You?"

"She's my daughter, isn't she? I'll lay out a few legal facts for the man. That ought to put the fear of God into him."

Hank grinned at her. "You would, too, wouldn't you?"

"Don't you laugh at me, Hank Robbins. Nobody messes with my family."

Hank put his arm around her. "What about you and me going together?" he suggested.

"Not without the rest of us," Harlan announced, joining them. "I've called Tate. I don't want it to be said that we've turned this into a lynching of an innocent man. The sheriff'll see to it that everything is taken care of nice and legal."

"I could have done that," Janet protested.

Harlan grinned at her. "Who are you kidding? You'd have been the first one to pop the man."

"Somebody has to stay here with Lizzy," Hank said.

"Melissa, Jenny and Sharon Lynn are on their way. Jenny's a heck of a shot if I do say so myself."

"Then we'll go as soon as they get here," Hank said, his expression grim. Come what may, he wanted this over. He wanted to start making plans with Lizzy for what promised to be the most unconventional marriage on record, at least for the next few years with her in Miami and him and their baby in Texas, and all of them chalking up enough frequent-flyer miles for a long honeymoon in Hawaii when it was over.

Lizzy awoke to the sight of her sister sitting at the window with a shotgun in her lap.

"Jenny?"

"Hey, sleepyhead. It's about time you woke up."

"What on earth is going on?"

Jenny glanced down as if surprised by the gun she was holding. "Oh, you mean this. Just a precaution."

Lizzy sat up slowly. "Maybe you'd better explain that."

"To tell you the truth, I'm not sure I understand all the details myself, but Daddy and Hank were convinced you might be in danger, so here I am. Melissa and Sharon Lynn are on guard downstairs."

"And the enemy is?"

"Brian."

Lizzy might have laughed, if it weren't so clear

that everyone else was taking this so seriously. "He wouldn't come here."

"I would have said the same thing a few days ago, but then I wouldn't have pegged him as an arsonist, either."

Lizzy's eyes widened. "They know for sure that he set the fire at Hank's?"

"Justin's convinced of it. He's got evidence he took to Tate and it must be pretty darned convincing because the sheriff's with the rest of them."

Lizzy moaned softly and covered her face with her hands.

"Lizzy? Sweetie, what is it? Are you okay? Is it the baby?"

"No, but this is all my fault. It started out with that stupid party."

"Don't be ridiculous," Jenny protested. "You are not to blame."

"Of course I am. I had to have my way. I had to make Hank fall in love with me, and look what a mess I've made of it. I'm pregnant and he's off chasing down a lunatic. If anything happens to him, I'll never forgive myself."

"Nothing is going to happen to Hank," Jenny said with confidence. She tilted her head. "So, when's the wedding?"

"Never. I can't marry him. It would be a disaster. I've been nothing but trouble for him."

"I don't think that's the way he sees it. He loves you, sweetie. There's no hiding from it."

Lizzy gave a sigh that was part dismay, part relief and wonder. "He really does, doesn't he?"

Jenny glanced out the window. "And here he comes now, all in one piece. I guess the battle is over and the good guys have won." She leaned down and brushed a kiss across Lizzy's forehead. "I'll give you two some privacy."

Lizzy clutched her hand. "No," she pleaded. "I can't see him yet."

"You don't have a choice. He's heading this way, and I, for one, am not about to stand in his way. Even with this gun in my hands, I'm no match for a man on a mission like this one."

Jenny took off just as Lizzy heard Hank taking the stairs two at a time. She heard them exchange a few murmured words in the hall, and then there was a sharp rap on her bedroom door.

"Lizzy? I know you're in there," Hank said. "I'm coming in."

She sighed and resigned herself to facing him. "The door's unlocked."

He opened it slowly and stepped inside. His face was haggard, as if he'd been getting no more sleep than she had been. The temptation to run to him was overwhelming, but she held back. To her dismay, she could already feel the faint stirring of resentment that because of him and their baby she was going to have to give up everything.

He walked over to the bed and sat beside her, not touching, but close enough that she could feel the heat from his body beckoning to her.

"Is everything over with Brian?"

"Tate has taken him in for questioning. There's enough evidence to lock him up."

"No shots fired?"

"Only one. Your daddy plugged the back tire on Brian's fancy sports car as he tried to get away."

"I'll bet the sleazeball loved that."

"He was madder about that than being taken into custody."

He leveled a look deep into her eyes then that had her squirming. "What's going on, Lizzy? It's not like you to hide out in your room."

"I had some thinking to do," she said.

Hank nodded. "Me, too."

Unable to stop herself, she reached out and pressed her hand against his stubbled cheek. "It looks as if all that thinking has been keeping you up at night."

He glanced sideways at her. "Doesn't seem to have affected you much. You're more beautiful than ever."

"You would say that even if I looked like something the cat dragged in," she teased. "You're just trying to have your way with me."

He grinned. "What if I am?"

She placed her hand over her belly, which was just showing the first signs of expanding to accommodate the baby growing inside. "Seems to me like you already have."

"Then a time or two more won't make any difference, will it?"

She regarded him indignantly. "A time or two?

And then what? Are you planning to get rid of me after that?''

He shook his head. ''Not willingly,'' he said quietly. ''Never willingly.''

''What then?''

''I'm giving you a gift,'' he said. ''A wedding gift, if you want it.''

''I haven't agreed to marry you yet.''

''Then think of the gift as a bribe.''

Lizzy sighed. ''Hank, you don't need to bribe me to marry you. I love you. I want to be your wife.''

''Maybe,'' he agreed. ''In due time. But the baby changed the timetable.''

''Just one of life's little unexpected surprises,'' she said, trying to keep her tone light, instead of bitter. ''Everyone always said I was the impetuous one. I ought to be able to handle this better than most.''

''But you're not handling it, darlin'. You're torn in two. I'm going to make it easy for you.''

Lizzy didn't like the sound of that. She didn't like it one little bit. She stood up and scowled at him.

''No,'' she said heatedly. ''You're not going to make it easy for me. That's what Daddy has done my whole life. If I wanted something, he got it for me. If I wanted to get into med school, he made it happen. If I wanted to have this baby on my own and turn it over to him and Janet or a nanny to raise, he'd make that happen too, but that's not the way it's going to be. This baby is my responsibility.''

''And mine,'' Hank reminded her fiercely. ''And

it's more than a responsibility, Lizzy. This baby is a miracle, our miracle.''

The anger went out of her at the wonder in his voice. When he opened his arms, this time she went to him and let herself be held.

"How could I have forgotten that, even for a minute?" she whispered against his neck. "How could I have forgotten what a blessing this is?"

"Because you have something to lose, darlin', something that's important to you. That's here and now, while the baby is still to come. It's harder to weigh them when one doesn't seem quite real yet. As for me, I'm getting the best of the bargain. I'm getting everything I ever dreamed of."

His gaze swept over her, and his lips curved into a tender smile. "You know, maybe we've been going about this all wrong. We've been looking at it as if it's an either-or situation. Somebody very wise once told me that the best marriages are based on compromise."

"Must not have been an Adams," Lizzy said dryly.

"Oh, but it was," he corrected, and the set to his jaw was every bit as stubborn as any Adams Lizzy had ever known.

"So, I've been thinking," he continued. "We could manage it if you stayed in Miami, but if you would transfer to medical school here in Texas, it'd be just around the corner."

Lizzy's heart began to fill with hope. "And what?

You'll take care of the baby? Is that what you're saying?"

Hank's chin jutted up a notch. "Why not?" he challenged. "It's better than hiring a nanny, which is what you'd have to do if the baby was with you in Miami. I suppose Mrs. Wyndham and I could manage to change a few diapers, assuming your daddy and Janet would let us near the baby."

Her spirits began to soar at the possibilities. "And I could come home and take over on the weekends. And maybe you could even bring the baby up for a few days, if we got an apartment near school with room for a nursery."

"It would take a lot of patience and flexibility on both our parts," Hank warned.

"But we could do it," Lizzy said. "I know we could." She peered into his eyes. "Hank, are you sure? Will you absolutely hate having me gone so much of the time?"

"I would hate it more if I lost you and the baby for good."

Lizzy was beginning to get the idea they could make it work. The prospect of actually marrying Hank without having to give up medicine actually took her breath away.

"We'd have to have a wedding before the end of summer," she said, then added with dismay, "There's not enough time. You know Daddy will want something elaborate."

"Oh, I think I can persuade him that expediency is more important than formality just this once,"

Hank said with confidence. "A little, old unexpected wedding won't throw him for a minute. As for you, you can just think of it as a surprise party and just show up on time."

Lizzy laughed and settled on his lap. "That gets us through the wedding, but Hank, what about later, after I get out of school?"

He leveled a gaze straight on her. "Now that's the solution you're going to have to come up with. I've done what I could to ease the way through the next few years."

Lizzy sighed and buried her face against his neck. Visions of a medical practice in a major trauma center paled by comparison to images of being with Hank and their child. A smile began to form. If Hank could compromise, so could she.

"Do you think Daddy'd be in the mood to build a hospital in Los Piños?" she asked. "That would be a whole lot nicer than having to go all the way to Garden City to work, especially if I've got a whole passel of kids around the house and a handsome husband I won't ever want to leave."

Hank laughed.

"Darlin', if it'll bring you home where you belong, I can flat out guarantee it. Heck, I'll raise the money for a wing myself." His expression sobered. "Think about it, though, Lizzy. I know you had your heart set on a big-city hospital. Can you be happy back in Los Piños?"

Lizzy gave the question the careful consideration Hank obviously expected. She'd always cared more about medicine than about the money. Maybe she was more like Marcus Welby and less like those *ER* doctors than she'd thought. She might not become a world-renowned trauma doctor in Los Piños, but the past few months had proven that Los Piños had its own share of emergencies. And when it came right down to it, family practice was looking awfully good to her, too.

"To an Adams, Los Piños will always be home," she said. "And you'll be here. And our children. That'll be enough excitement for me." She would make it enough, because Hank was giving her so much in return, not just his love, but his understanding.

"Children?" he was saying now, his expression hopeful.

She grinned at him. "I have a feeling once we get started, Mr. Robbins, we're not going to want to stop."

"A whole new dynasty," he whispered. "A Robbins dynasty. I think I like the sound of that."

"Don't tell Daddy that," Lizzy warned. "To him every baby in this family is an Adams, no matter what last name they might carry."

"I won't begrudge him that much," Hank said. "After all, he is giving me the woman he thinks of as his own precious miracle."

"Giving?" Lizzy repeated. "The man has practically shoved me into your arms."

"But I was more than ready to catch you, darlin'. And now that I have, I don't intend to ever let you go."

* * * * *

Watch for the sexy, emotionally wounded
lawbreaker who steals Justin's heart in
NATURAL BORN LAWMAN,
coming next month from
Silhouette Special Edition.

$Silhouette$®SPECIAL EDITION®

Newfound sisters Bliss, Tiffany and Katie
learn more about family and true love
than they *ever* expected.

A new miniseries by
LISA JACKSON

A FAMILY KIND OF GUY (SE#1191) August 1998
Bliss Cawthorne wanted nothing to do with ex-flame
Mason Lafferty, the cowboy who had destroyed her
dreams of being his bride. Could Bliss withstand his irresistible charm—the second time around?

A FAMILY KIND OF GAL (SE#1207) November 1998
How could widowed single mother Tiffany Santini be
attracted to her sexy brother-in-law, J.D.? Especially
since J.D. was hiding something that could destroy the
love she had just found in his arms....

And watch for the conclusion of this series in
early 1999 with Katie Kinkaid's story in
A FAMILY KIND OF WEDDING.

Available at your favorite retail outlet. Only from

MEN at WORK

All work and no play?
Not these men!

October 1998
SOUND OF SUMMER by Annette Broadrick

Secret agent Adam Conroy's seductive gaze could hypnotize a woman's heart. But it was Selena Stanford's body that needed saving— when she stumbled into the middle of an espionage ring and forced Adam out of hiding....

November 1998
GLASS HOUSES by Anne Stuart

Billionaire Michael Dubrovnik never lost a negotiation—until Laura de Kelsey Winston changed the boardroom rules. He might acquire her business...but a kiss would cost him his heart....

December 1998
FIT TO BE TIED by Joan Johnston

Matthew Benson had a way with words and women—but he refused to be tied down. Could Jennifer Smith get him to retract his scathing review of her art by trying another tactic: tying him *up*?

Available at your favorite retail outlet!

MEN AT WORK™

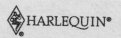

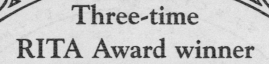

COMING NEXT MONTH

#1213 THEIR CHILD—Penny Richards
That's My Baby!

Horse breeder Drew McShane had selflessly married pregnant ranching heiress Kim Campion to give her baby a name. As their darling daughter illuminated their lives, Drew began to realize how much he truly adored Hannah's mommy. Could he convince his wary wife they were destined for love?

#1214 HEART OF THE HUNTER—Lindsay McKenna
Morgan's Mercenaries: The Hunters

He never let anything—or anyone—get to him. But when Captain Reid Hunter's latest mission meant guarding Dr. Casey Morrow, it irked him that the feisty beauty fought him every step of the way. Now her achingly tender kisses might turn this world-weary cynic into a true believer in love!

#1215 DR. DEVASTATING—Christine Rimmer
Prescription: Marriage

Devastatingly handsome Dr. Derek Taylor had inspired many of nurse Lee Murphy's fantasies. Suddenly all her secret yearnings sprang to life when the dashing doc began paying an awful lot of attention to little old mousy her! Could it be that sometimes dreams *do* come true?

#1216 NATURAL BORN LAWMAN—Sherryl Woods
And Baby Makes Three: The Next Generation

Justin Adams was a by-the-book lawman—no exceptions. Until the day he caught a desperate Patsy Longhorn swiping a bottle of baby medicine for her feverish tyke. After taking the penniless mother and son under his protective wing, the softhearted sheriff vowed to safeguard their future—with him!

#1217 WIFE IN THE MAIL—Marie Ferrarella

Shayne Kerrigan was in quite a quandary! His irresponsible brother had run off—and the lonely widower had to break the news to his sibling's jilted mail-order bride. All too soon, Shayne and his children were under sweet Sydney's spell. Could Shayne convince her to become *his* Christmas bride?

#1218 THE SECRET DAUGHTER—Jackie Merritt
The Benning Legacy

A lifetime ago Blythe Benning had bid goodbye to her college love—as well as their beloved baby. Now Brent Morrison was back, eager to rekindle their passion—and to locate the daughter he'd never met. But when their quest unearthed a shattering family secret, it seemed their lives might never be the same....